The Chameleon Soul Mate

The Worlds Apart Series

Evelyn Lederman

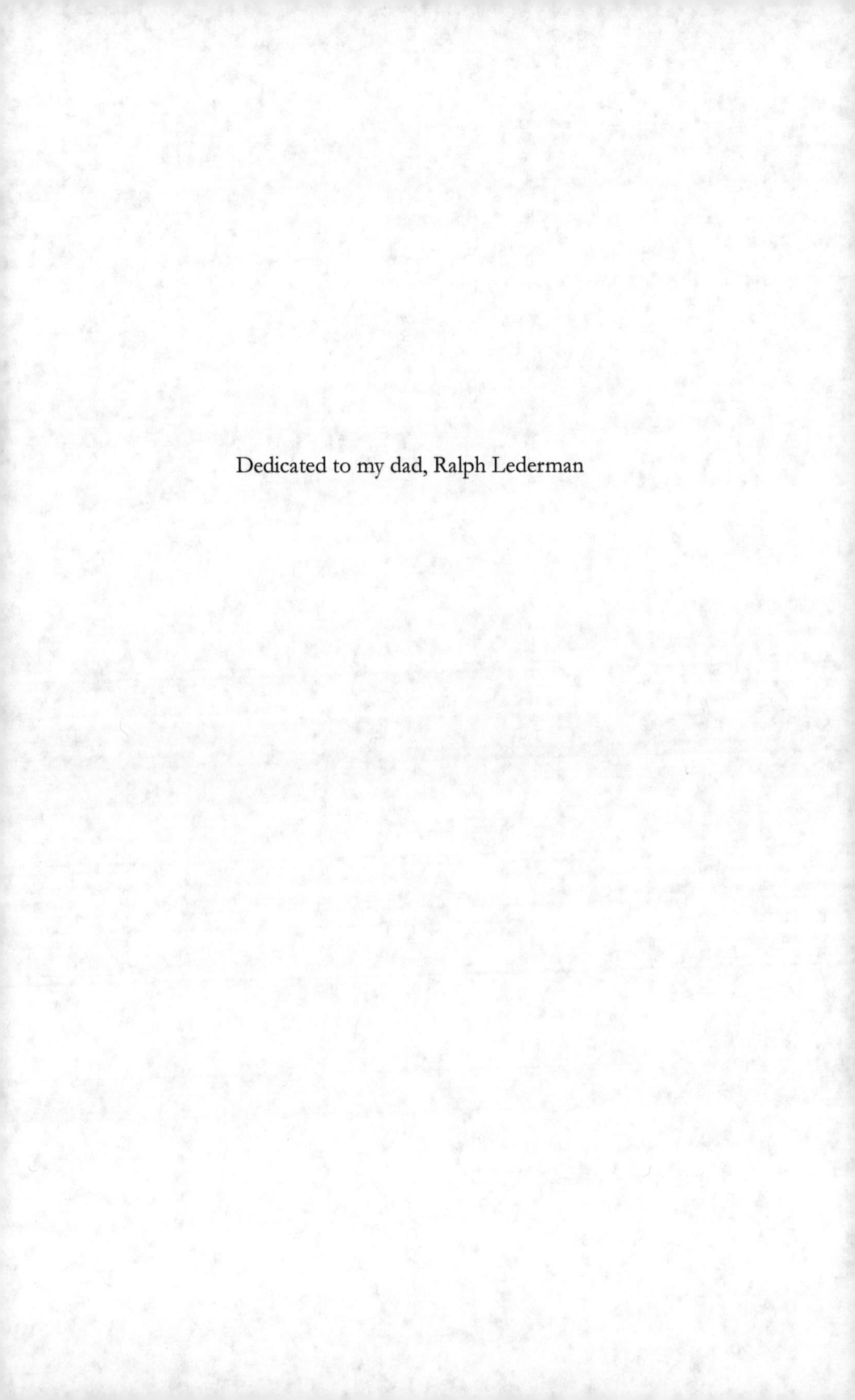

Dedicated to my dad, Ralph Lederman

Acknowledgements:

~

To Michele Callahan, founder of the RomCon Convention. Through attendance at Romcon, I have been introduced to the incredible community of romance writers and readers.

To my editor, Tina Winograd. For making this a better book. The woman loves conflict!

To V.A. Dold, my good friend. Thank you for all your support and the zillion questions you answered.

Chapter 1

~

Arizona

Alexandra Mann, 'Alex' to friends and foes, disconnected from the call center system and let out a long, painful sigh. People never called to comment on how great things were, just to complain.

But she had the ability to stay calm under pressure and deal with any situation. Didn't matter if it was a customer yelling or her two best friends coming to her with their latest crisis. Alex took whatever life threw at her and made lemon drop cocktails.

Finally, Friday was here and Alex was going up to Sedona with three friends. They had been planning this trip for five months, and the countdown was finally over. This weekend was a double celebration: her twenty-first birthday and her best friend Shirl's twenty-third.

She had actually taken a half day of vacation so she and Shirl could get a jump on the traffic that headed north every Friday afternoon. Two of her co-workers were joining them, but had to work all day and would drive up later.

She grabbed her purse and pulled out her phone. The display showed that Shirley Tomlinson called. Shirl, as she liked to be called, had grown up with Alex at a local Phoenix orphanage. Although Alex was younger than Shirl, they were best friends and as close as sisters. Shirl and Candy, who also grew up with them at the orphanage, were Alex's only family. The three were connected, at times it felt like they could read each other's minds.

Alex had given up on the dream of a real family long before the orphanage stopped parading her in front of perspective parents. Years of couples talking and playing with her, only to have them walk away, had taken their toll. The disappointment she felt at the continual rejection caused her to cry herself to sleep on many occasions. She would find herself blending into the shadows in order not to be passed over again.

To this day, she had a tendency to blend into the background. Her best friends were always in the spotlight, where Alex tended to be invisible in their presence. Shirl was tall, blond, and stop traffic gorgeous. Candy, on the other hand, had a self-confidence that made her radiant. When they were together, both men and women would flock to Candy.

Having left her cubical, Alex took the opportunity to listen to Shirl's voice mail message. "Alex, it's Shirl. I've got a killer migraine and I can't make it to Sedona this weekend."

If anyone else had canceled on her, she would have been angry. However, she knew Shirl got terrible migraines that would down a small elephant. It seemed as though the headaches were growing in frequency and she was concerned about her friend. Alex recently started having migraines herself. She and Shirl were so close, she felt they were probably sympathy headaches.

When Alex reached the call center's lobby, she called Shirl before she walked out into the Arizona heat.

"What?" Shirl growled as the call connected.

"How are you feeling? Do you need anything?" Alex asked.

"Can you get me a new brain?"

"Doubtful, but I'll look into it. I am so sorry you won't make it to Sedona with us."

"I know, Alex," Shirl's voice began to fade. "Candy will stop by before she takes her class on this weekend's field trip. Don't worry, I will be fine."

Shirl hung up before Alex could say anything more. Alex placed her phone in her purse and walked toward her car in the stifling Arizona heat. The car was all packed and ready to go for the trip up to Sedona. Since she was not picking up Shirl, she immediately got on I-17 and headed north.

Alex loved Sedona and started thinking about what types of adventures she'd have this weekend. Something unusual always happened when she was there. It was odd, she was never able to put into words what she experienced. Some invisible force always seemed to draw her.

⌒⌒

Alex made good time. Leaving Phoenix early afternoon was the trick, beating the hordes of commuters heading home after work. She headed straight to her hotel.

It would be some time before her call center friends would join her. In the meantime, Alex had time to hike in Boynton Canyon. She opened her suitcase, pulled out a T-shirt and shorts.

The Boynton Canyon Vortex was one of the four vortexes that contributed to the energy felt throughout Sedona. Alex generally hiked Boynton Canyon because she felt the best energy there and enjoyed the trails. A lot was written about Sedona's vortexes, including the belief the energy was the result of inter-dimensional gateways. She did not believe all that nonsense, but her friend Shirl certainly did. With that thought, Alex felt the loss of Shirl not being there. She could almost visualize her friend standing next to her, clutching her crystal necklaces.

She walked to her car and made the short trip between the hotel and Boynton Canyon. The parking lot closest to the trail was packed. Fortunately, she had the world's smallest car and found a spot where someone had parked badly, leaving only three quarters of a space. She easily fit into the spot and patted the dashboard of her beloved car. It was fire engine red, with a white racing stripe down the side. She loved zipping around town in it.

Alex changed from her sneakers into her hiking boots, locked the car and made her way to the trail head. She loved the sound her boots made against the gravel trail. Alex had just purchased a new pair of hiking boots as a birthday present to herself. The boots almost came up a quarter of her leg and were kind of clunky. She was not going to take any chances if she came across a snake along the trail.

Although the lot had been full, she didn't see anyone on the trail. A flash of light caught her eye. It was the reflection coming off a bracelet worn by someone suddenly ahead of her. Her eyes left the cuff bracelet to the man who wore it. He was tall with blond hair, and she couldn't help but admire his body.

The man was oddly dressed for hiking. It appeared he was wearing a tunic and leggings. He had broad shoulders underneath the blue tunic and the leggings were molded to his powerful legs. She could see the muscle definition of his legs even from this distance. He must have decided to take a little hike before performing in a Shakespearean play. Sedona was known for supporting all art forms.

Alex admired his body, but unfortunately her body was not reacting to his. It never did, regardless how attractive she found the man. Oddly, Shirl and Candy had the same problem. She dated, because girls her age dated. She had not been with a man in over six months. Every relationship was disappointing when it became physical. The guys she dated didn't want to sustain a relationship if they had to deal with an ice queen in bed.

As she continued on the path, she kept an eye on the man, closing the gap between them. He was carrying a number of sacks that seemed to slow him down. Another oddity about the man. Who carried sacks on a day hike, rather than a backpack?

He was in her sight one minute and the next he vanished. Where did he go? Alex ran forward, thinking the man had fallen and needed help. She arrived at the spot where she had last seen him and there was no sign of him.

An invisible force pulled her forward off her feet. She screamed, as the motion continued and her vision went black. Her lungs seized and she fell into what she could only think was an endless void.

Chapter 2

~

The Troyk Universe, Aster Province

Tarsea Childers patiently waited for Darden to emerge through the portal. It was actually quite peaceful not having to listen to anyone talking or pushing thoughts through any of the many telepathic channels he had to manage continually. They were too far from the city for the communal pathways to reach him. He often wondered what it would be like to live in a world where the population was not telepathic. What peace that would provide, not constantly deluged with conversations.

He loved taking the hike up the mountain to where the natural gateway between worlds existed. Aster Province buildings were made of stone and surrounded by purple flowering trees, shrubs, and flowers. Unlike the city, the trail had a variety of blooming flowers that differed from the purple that dominated the Troyk city. Here nature showed the true variety of colors, scents and densities a world should possess. He looked down the valley where the city was nestled. Since Aster Province was surrounded by mountains, the pollen trapped in the valley painted the sky violet.

Darden Lours walked through the portal. "Thanks for meeting me," he greeted Tarsea.

"Glad you are back. How were the headaches?" Tarsea was always relieved when his best friend returned home from whatever parallel universe he visited. As of late, it seemed to be only Ginkgo Terra. Very few gatherers were willing to go to Ginkgo Terra due to the impact the planet's atmosphere had on their telepathic brains. Gatherers early on complained of headaches they experienced in that world.

"Nothing I cannot handle. The herbs I take have helped." Darden became a very successful gatherer because he would venture to that universe and return with the ginkgo herb their world required. His friend had shared with Tarsea that he had found other herbs that would minimize the headaches. He did not share this knowledge with the other gatherers, wanting exclusive rights to Ginkgo Terra. The additional herbs were always given to Tarsea's mother Leenea. She would blend them with other herbs and create a tea that helped them better manage the telepathic channels.

They were about to start down the mountain when there was a terrible scream and both men turned to the portal as the most beautiful woman Tarsea had ever laid eyes on fell through. At the sight of her, he felt like he had been punched in the stomach. It was as if he had the wind knocked out of him. Darden was the quicker of the two of them and caught her. Tarsea stood like a fool watching.

The girl continued to scream in Darden's arms as he tried to calm her. "By the Prime!" Darden exclaimed. "What are you doing here, Alexandra?"

It was obvious his friend knew the girl. Tarsea wanted to help aid in quieting her. He used the name Darden had. "Alexandra, you need to stop screaming! Take a breath and let it out slowly, you are starting to hyperventilate."

As they were trying to calm the girl, he telepathically asked his friend questions. *"Who is she? How do you know her? What is she to you?"* For some reason that last question was the most important to him.

Darden talked to the girl, ignoring his questions. Tarsea figured he would have to wait for his answers until after the girl stopped screaming.

Tarsea stared at the creature in Darden's arms. She had the most beautiful light auburn hair that shimmered in the sun. The girl had bright green eyes that showed terror, although he felt under normal circumstances they would show intelligence. Her skin was like a luminous pearl, she almost glowed a light pink. She was slight. Tarsea had the odd thought he wanted to feed her, so there would be more of her for him to touch. His fingers ached to touch her skin and slide his whole being into her body. He had never reacted to anyone in this manner.

Alex heard a voice break through the screams, which she finally realized was coming from her. She took a breath and looked into the deep blue eyes of the blond man she had been following. Alex concentrated on bringing down her heart rate and controlling her breathing.

"Alexandra, can I touch you to make sure you are unhurt?" the man holding her asked when he noted she had calmed down. She was about to respond when she heard a growl. Alex looked in the direction of the sound.

There stood what Alex could only call was the most striking man she had ever seen. His face was full of angles, as if an artist chiseled it from marble. He was dark, with a deep tan and short black hair. Like the man she had followed, he too wore a tunic and leggings. He was all in black. The expression on his face was that of surprise, then confusion. She took it that he normally did not growl.

Alex wiggled out of the blonde's arms as he released his hold on her. She slowly got up and patted herself down, checking to see if she was hurt. It appeared she was fine. She looked around to get her bearings and stopped cold. The sky had a violet hue to it, and she was no longer in Boynton Canyon. Alex staggered and the blonde steadied her.

"Alexandra, are you all right?" he asked as he continued to hold her shoulder and helped her balance. Although she appreciated the support, she had no idea where she was or who these men were. She could not understand how they knew her name.

"I don't know, am I?" a very confused Alex answered him. "How do you know me? Who are you and why is the sky violet?" She knew she sounded shaky, primarily because she was. It surprised her that although the situation terrified her, she was not afraid of these men. That made no sense whatsoever. She decided to go with that feeling for her own sanity. After all, he had been very gentle when he held her.

"Alexandra, I promise I will tell you everything," the blonde said. "But we have to go now! The patrols may be on their way after a second body came through the portal. You must have been caught in the stream before the portal closed."

The blonde eyed his friend, then turned back to Alex. "My name is Darden, the man with the scowl is Tarsea."

The mention of patrols made Alex tense, a reaction she noticed she shared with the men. Her eyes kept going back to the man with the scowl. What would have happened if they had not been there and the patrol had found her? These men had been so nice to her.

As she saw it, she had three choices. Her first was to escape from these men and try to fall through another portal home. That option did not look too promising since she did not know how the portal worked.

Choice number two was to trust these men and go with them. She certainly did not like the sound of a patrol coming to check out what followed Darden through the portal.

Her last option was to ask the men to open the portal to Earth and she would go through it. Alex did not know if she could handle another trip through so soon. For the time being, she would go with these men. However, she would not rule out them opening the portal for her if the opportunity arose.

Alex nodded as she continued to stare at Tarsea. He had the most incredible greenish brown eyes she had ever seen. They bore through her with what she could only think was a possessive gaze.

Before she looked away, he shifted his eyes to Darden. It appeared they were having a silent argument. A wave of dizziness rolled over her. She leaned against a tree as the men continued their strange interchange.

Tarsea watched Alexandra as he continued to converse with Darden, through the telepathic channel both men shared. He needed answers to who the girl was.

He was a player with a well-known reputation, but this girl drew him in a way he never experienced in his life.

Tarsea was anxious for answers. *"I want to know everything now, including who she is and what she means to you."*

"Her name is Alexandra Mann," Darden telepathically communicated. *"She is the daughter of one of the couples who left with Benko Jarlyn. Her parents are dead, but Benko is still alive. I have found my soul mate in the Ginkgo Terra Universe, she is Benko's daughter Cassandra."*

Tarsea stopped breathing mid-breath and stared at Darden. He did not know how to react to what he just heard. His senses and mind had been already in overdrive due to Alexandra.

Benko Jarlyn was the son of the current ruler of the Troyk Universe. He had tried to overthrow his tyrannical father, only to disappear through the portal over twenty years ago.

If the information about Benko Jarlyn was not enough, the possibility that soul mates really existed added hope to the dreams he did not know he had, until he saw Alexandra.

"Hello, I am still here," Alexandra said. "I want to know where I am and what is going on!" She had her hands on her hips, her foot tapping impatiently. Alexandra's small chin lifted in defiance. The girl was absolutely adorable.

"Alexandra," Tarsea addressed her, "we will answer all your questions. However, as Darden said, we have to get out of here." They had spent too much time talking. If a patrol had been sent, they had little time left for further discussion.

She looked at them, behind her toward the invisible portal and then back to them. "But I want to go home," Alexandra stated, "back to Sedona. Can't I go back the way I came?"

Tarsea's heart dropped at the words Alexandra uttered. How was he going to keep her here? He had just found her and was not going to lose her without a fight. From his intense reaction to her, he knew she was his soul mate.

Darden placed his hands on her shoulders. "Alexandra, the headaches that Shirley suffers, there is a reason for them. The world where Sedona is, it is not your world. Your parents were from this world. Your adopted universe attacks our telepathic brains when we reach our mid-twenties, which is what triggers headaches. I cannot have you go back just to suffer and ultimately die like your parents. Again, we need to leave. We cannot afford to have you fall into the wrong hands. Please, you have to trust us." Darden released her shoulders and stepped back.

Tarsea watched the color drain from Alexandra's face. Her chin fell as her shoulders slumped. He missed the fiery little minx with her chin up high. Her surrender broke his heart.

Alex nodded. At this point she was not sure what to believe, it was all so surreal. He knew both her and Shirl, knew of their headaches. On top of everything else, he told her Earth was not her world. None of this made any sense. She was numb.

All those articles that Shirl read and told Alex about, were swimming through her head. She said Sedona's four vortexes led to an existence beyond our perception. The fact it was true and she was there, blew her mind.

Except for the purple sky, it all looked so normal. She could have been on any hiking trail, although she did not recognize a number of the plants that bordered the trail. She looked down upon a city unknown to her, a city littered with trees of different shades of purple.

She decided to trust these men. There was a connection with Tarsea she could not explain. She looked at him, and her body hummed. A reaction she had never felt.

They started down the mountain trail. Alex glanced at Tarsea. He was beautiful beyond belief and he made her very nervous in a sexual way. It felt like butterflies were swarming in her stomach. She wanted him to touch her, but the prospect terrified her. He was a head shorter than Darden, but was powerfully built. She was mesmerized by the way he moved. He had the grace and power of a panther. Alex could imagine touching and tasting him all over, the sooner the better.

Alex was ripped from her thoughts as a bout of nausea hit her. She struggled to continue walking.

Tarsea was enjoying the view. He liked the way Alexandra's hips swayed as she trudged down the mountain. She was a little thing, but he saw she was fit. Her legs shapely and muscular. He found it humorous how such a pixie could lift her legs with such big boots on her feet. His eyes roamed her body again. She had a great ass, he could not wait to hold those cheeks in his hands as he drove into her. Her hair went to the midpoint of her back. Tarsea watched how the sun brought out different shades of auburn. When it hit just right, her hair shone like a wave of fire cascading down her back.

He had been with many women over the years, but Tarsea had never been immediately attracted body and soul as he had with Alexandra. It surprised him, the feral reaction he had when Darden touched her. He generally did not growl like an animal. When Darden had communicated he had found his soul mate in the other world, the violence he felt within simmered to a low flame.

Tarsea watched as Alexandra faltered and then fall forward. "Darden," he called out, "she is falling."

Darden turned, but was not fast enough to catch her before she came down hard on the trail. She tumbled a couple of feet before his friend scooped her up.

"Portal sickness, I was expecting this. She was dragged behind me into the portal and had a rough ride."

"We should take her to my parents' house. I will contact Koel to back us up as we come off the mountain and make our way through the city." Tarsea's parents had a spacious house, he could not take her to his small apartment.

There were a multitude of communal pathways that everyone could link into. In addition, familial pathways existed between those who shared the same blood. A unique communal pathway had developed between Tarsea and Darden several years ago. Since then, three others had been able to link into this strange channel. Koel, Darden's cousin, was one.

"Koel," Tarsea linked into the pathway. *"Meet me and Darden at the bottom of the portal trail."*

Tarsea studied the unconscious Alexandra in his friend's arms. "We need to cover her, Darden. She is not wearing a clan bracelet. Her clothes are all wrong and will raise a number of questions as we walk through the streets."

He generally carried a large sack when he met Darden at the portal. Tarsea spread it over Alexandra, careful not to have any physical contact with her. Physical contact would immediately indicate if Alexandra was his soul mate. He was both hopeful and terrified to know if it was true.

They had not taken more than a dozen steps when Tarsea saw the patrol officer on his way up the mountain. Time had run out.

Chapter 3

~

Tarsea saw the distance between them and the patrol officer narrow with each step they took. Generally, one or two patrol officers were sent to investigate activity around the portal.

"Shit!" Darden swore under his breath, "It is Narmouth, a real hard ass. We are in serious trouble. There is no way he is going to let us take Alexandra anywhere other than The Palace."

The Aster Province Palace was the center most building in the city. It was the seat of government, home of their Prime Ruler Jeryl Jarlyn, and where all non-authorized portal travelers were sent. Jeryl Jarlyn was obsessed with finding his traitorous son, his companions, and any offspring they may have had. Alexandra was exactly who they were looking for.

"Greetings," Raine Narmouth said. "I will escort you to The Palace. Looks like you have someone the Prime Ruler will love to meet." Tarsea did not like the way Narmouth was eyeing Alexandra.

"She did not come through the portal," Tarsea informed the officer. "We heard her fall further up the trail after Darden came through. We are taking her to my parents' to recover."

"I do not think so," Narmouth sneered, "she is going to The Palace. Your story can be confirmed by an intelligence officer after we are done interviewing everyone."

Tarsea was just about to argue with Narmouth, when he saw Koel coming up the trail behind the patrol officer. Koel was carrying a fairly large rock and proceeded to bash the officer's skull.

"That was a rocking good time!" Koel laughed. "It should be good for a three day memory lapse." Most head injuries resulted in short term memory loss. Any memories during the lapse were unrecoverable.

"Good job," Tarsea said to Koel. "Get Starc up here and work on a cover story for when Narmouth wakes. We are heading to my parents' house." Starc was Darden's twin, also a patrol officer.

"Who is the little beauty?" Koel inquired.

"Long story," Tarsea answered. "Come to my parents' house tonight and we will go over everything."

"Anything for you, sweetheart!" Koel said, as he winked in his direction.

Tarsea shook his head at Koel. Darden's cousin was a clown, but a tactical genius. Half the time Tarsea had to hold himself back from slugging the guy.

They continued down the path, leaving the unconscious patrol officer with Koel. Their new challenge was walking through the city, carrying an unconscious girl without getting stopped.

The streets of Aster Province were teaming with activity, since the second day of each new moon brought out the vendors. Tarsea navigated through the crowds, as Darden carried the unconscious girl. Occasionally he turned to see if Alexandra was all right. She was bleeding from a wound on her leg and was trailing blood. It was certainly not a lot of blood, but it still disturbed Tarsea.

He was surprised there were so few inquiries through the communal channels about what happened to her or who she was. It appeared his neighbors were more concerned about getting the best bargain at each stall.

Tarsea continued to wind through the streets. The breeze had picked up and purple blossoms were littering his path. He sent his parents an update on their progress, using the familial link.

When they arrived at the house he grew up in, his mother opened the door as he was reaching for the doorknob. She ushered them in and guided their party to the central common room. Darden gently placed Alexandra on the couch.

"She has portal sickness," Darden explained to Tarsea's mother. "She should be out for several more hours." Tarsea was not sure if he had told his mother Alexandra's condition, when he communicated through their familial link.

His mother looked at the girl. "She is bleeding, let me clean her up. This little girl will be fine here with me. I believe you all have places you need to be."

Tarsea knew his mother was referring to him. He generally spent his days at The Palace, attending Prime Council meetings. The Prime Council was the legislative branch of the Troyk government. He supported a number of representatives, researching and recommending how to vote on bills before the chamber.

"You are right, Mom, as always," Tarsea said as he kissed her cheek. "I will be back around six tonight. Alexandra will be waking about then."

He also had plans with his girlfriend this afternoon. Tarsea used a variety of girls over the years as a cover for his anti-governmental activities. He had not expected he would have to explain his former dating habits to a soul mate.

Chapter 4

Tarsea made his way to the Aster Province Palace. The four story Palace was the tallest building, allowing its ruling class vistas of the city they were elected to serve. No other buildings were allowed to be more than two stories tall.

He proceeded to the second floor, where the Prime Representatives met. Tarsea entered the chamber, while Prime Marcete continued on about the benefits of mind control on the general populace of the Aster Province. The mind control faction took over leadership of the government twenty-five years ago. Aster Province was the gem of the Troyk world.

Jeryl Jarlyn was the Prime Ruler and leader of the mind control movement. Throughout his reign, various uprisings occurred to outlaw the use of mind control. Jeryl's own son, Benko Jarlyn, led the first campaign. Tarsea had secretly supported the latest peaceful uprisings against Jeryl. He would support Benko, if he ever returned. The news that Benko was alive, made his return more of a reality than a dream.

Prime Hosp took the floor, to support the words that were just communicated to the body of Primes. However, Tarsea knew Rance Hosp did not believe the nonsense he was spouting. Rance supported the secret factions that wanted to eliminate mind control usage. Most government officials that wanted change had one or two contacts they used. This reduced the threat of discovery.

Tarsea was Rance's only secret anti-government contact. He came from, what appeared to be a strong government supporting family. No one would think twice about Rance meeting with Tarsea. His father had secretly supported Benko's cause all those years ago and continued to quietly support other factions that arose over time. Tarsea, his brother Tolfer, Darden, Starc, and Koel were currently involved in a faction that worked to bring about peaceful change.

Their primary role was to help dissidents escape through the portal, when it became too dangerous for them to remain. It was frustrating how little progress they had made over the years. They were all committed to a peaceful change. However, Tarsea saw the attraction of a more violent approach, bringing about faster change. He continually struggled over getting involved in the quicker solution.

"Rance speaks too eloquently," his brother Tolfer commented using their special telepathic pathway he shared with his brother and his friends.

His brother's presence and words ripped him from the inappropriate thoughts he was having. Lately he had more of these feelings and had to keep reminding himself, he supported only peaceful change.

"Rance needs to be convincing," Tarsea informed his brother. *"He has to be seen as a supporter of mind control in order not to draw attention to himself. It is best for him to blend in with all the other primes."*

Tarsea looked at his watch. *"I will see you later,"* he told his brother. *"I have to meet Chartail. Make sure to be at our parents' house by six."*

"You have had a busy day, brother. I will be there."

Tarsea left the chamber and headed to meet his girlfriend. He had been seeing Chartail Adholm for seven months. She was the daughter of Prime Adholm, a staunch advocate of Jeryl Jarlyn. Seeing Chartail was another means to strengthen the illusion that he supported mind control and the current group in power.

Prime Adholm possessed the ability to enter someone's mind and impact how they thought and acted. Fortunately, Chartail did not inherit that ability. It would have been too dangerous to pursue a relationship with her if that had been the case.

Yet again, he thought of Alexandra, who lay unconscious in his parents' home. He exchanged one girl for another on a regular basis, but never really thought how that impacted the last girl he dumped. His relationships were a front, but he worried about how she would react to his dating and sexual history.

Aster Province had neighborhood meeting places scattered throughout the city. Each meeting place had a park in the middle, with multiple walking paths. The meeting places were flanked by restaurants and bars. Children could play, while their parents enjoyed a glass of wine. The younger crowd tended to gravitate to the covered bars, farther away from park entrances.

Tarsea walked through the crowded meeting place bar. His eyes surveyed the area and he found where Chartail was holding court. She really was stunning with her long blond hair, tanned skin, and her coltish legs. How different Alexandra was from this woman and the women he had dated in the past. His mind kept going back to the woman he met this afternoon.

Chartail was in mid-sentence in her conversation with one of the many men who surrounded her. She turned in Tarsea's direction and smiled when they made eye contact. He made his way to where she stood. Chartail kissed him and her taste lingered on his lips. He wondered how Alexandra tasted.

"You are late!" Chartail complained. "I will forgive you if you buy me another drink."

She spoke out loud since they only shared the communal pathway. Married couples would eventually link into their spouse's familial pathways with continual proximity and fluid exchanges. Tarsea thought there must be something very intimate about talking directly to one's soul mate, a channel that only they shared. He ached for such intimacy with Alexandra, if she was his soul mate, as he suspected.

"I am sorry," Tarsea said, as he telepathically ordered Chartail another drink. "I was at the Prime Council meeting. Prime Hosp was speaking and I did not want to miss it."

"Did my father speak?" Chartail inquired. She never went to the assembly to hear her father or any of the prime representatives' debate issues.

"Oh, yes," Tarsea laughed. "When does your father not take the opportunity to praise his fellow prime members and voice support within the chamber?" Her father was a real windbag. Fortunately his daughter did not take after him in that manner.

Chartail returned his laughter and kissed Tarsea again.

"It is time to head to your parents' home," Koel communicated to Tarsea. *"Thought I would stop by in case you got tied up. The other business has been taken care of."* Tarsea wondered how difficult Raine Narmouth was once he woke.

"I have to go," Tarsea told Chartail. "Koel and I have research to do for an upcoming bill." His friend showing up provided him a convenient excuse to leave the bar. Koel was always good with the details that Tarsea sometimes missed.

Chartail did not appear happy that he had to leave. "You work too much," she pouted. "It seems a waste that you have to leave and miss all the fun."

Tarsea for the time being felt he needed to pacify this woman. "I will see you later," he whispered in her ear. "How about we meet here after you get off work tomorrow. I will buy you dinner to make up for having to leave tonight. We can go to your favorite restaurant." That seemed to pacify her.

Tarsea paid for Chartail's drink and met Koel at the entrance to the park. They headed to his parents' house. Alexandra should be waking any time now.

Chapter 5

Alex woke slowly from the nightmare she had just had. She was still a little nauseous and there was a lot of static in her head.

"Alexandra," she heard a man say, "are you awake?"

She moaned and through the fog tried to place where she had heard that voice before.

Alex woke with a start, she had heard that voice in her nightmare. She opened her eyes and saw the black haired man looking at her with his beautiful greenish brown eyes. Her nightmare was a reality!

"Relax," Tarsea said, "we are at my parents' house. You are recovering from what we call portal sickness."

Alex looked around. She recognized Tarsea and Darden, but there were a number of people she did not know hovering around. Tarsea must have picked up on her anxiety, since he turned and looked at all the people behind him. She did not hear him say anything, but everyone but the two older people backed out of her sight.

"Alexandra," Tarsea said, "this is my mother, Leenea. Beside her is my father, Zane Childers."

All right, these were his parents, she could handle this. She nodded to them and tried to smile.

The nausea was passing, but the static in her ears was getting worse.

Zane extended his hand to her. "Welcome," he said, as he took her hand. "You are an honored guest in our home, Alexandra. We hope to make your transition to our world as comfortable as possible."

She looked up into the same greenish brown eyes, he had passed on to his son. Alex was too overwhelmed to say anything. They were yet again, talking about her being in another world.

"Welcome to the Troyk Universe," his mother said. "This is where your parents were from. We are a telepathic people, conversing through many pathways or channels. In time you will learn to use these pathways. However, in the meantime, we will speak out loud."

Alex remembered Darden had mentioned her parents on the mountain. "My parents?" She had no memories of either her mother or father.

"There is good, as well as bad, in our world," Leenea continued. "As I am sure was true of your adopted home. Before you were born, a group took power that wished to control the people of this universe with their ability to practice mind control. Many people opposed this, including your parents. They left through the portal to escape the consequences of their actions."

Alex stared at Leenea. If she had not experienced the black void portal and the violet sky, she would have thought these people were crazy. Her parents were from a parallel dimension and now she was there?

"How?" Alex asked. That was all she was able to communicate at this point.

"I am a crystal telepath, like Shirl's mother," Darden said. "Through my mind, I control the gateways between worlds, using crystals. I have visited your home on many occasions and learned of your existence, as well as your friends. Your planet's atmosphere is toxic to our brain chemistry and caused the aneurysms that killed your parents."

"I don't understand, how did you know about me and Shirl?"

"I came across Benko Jarlyn several years ago and have been working with him to bring you and your friends here. Shirl is in worse shape, so I planned to bring her over first. You have an aunt in the next province and we planned to unite you with your family."

"If what you are saying is true, why did they stay on Earth?" Alex was trying to shoot holes in their story. It all seemed so unreal, like something you'd read in a science fiction novel. Plus, they dangled a relative before her, as you would dangle a carrot in front of a horse.

"We call Earth, Ginkgo Terra. Shirl's mother died before they realized it was the air that was toxic. She was their only crystal telepath, so they were stranded. Benko believes he survived because he was the only mind control telepath in the group and had an immunity to what was killing his friends."

The static in Alex's head was getting worse and Darden was talking nonsense.

"What you are saying is crazy!" Alex shouted. She needed to get a grip on things, think logically. The static kept getting louder and louder and it was more difficult to think.

"Why are things so different, yet so similar? Plus, you are speaking English, how is that even possible?"

There was a momentary silence. She really got them with that one. Let's see how they explained that away.

"Imagine the existence of infinite universes," Zane said. "Each having fractured off one another. A world can result from multiple fractures, with the people and places slightly modified as each division occurs. Our world must have fractured off yours, with at least one of the languages carrying over. Through one or more fractures, our world lost a lot of the land masses that Darden tells us your adopted home has. We have also been able to tap into parts of our brains that the people of your adopted universe have not, our telepathic abilities."

This was all too much! Alex could feel panic building, as the static got louder and louder. She felt as if her brain was going to explode.

Tarsea watched Alexandra's reactions as more information was being shared. He did not think she could take much more before she broke.

"Please, stop!" Alexandra cried. "I can't handle any more of this." She placed her head in her hands and brought her head to her knees.

Tarsea had to forget about holding back physical contact, he could not stand back any more and watch her suffer. He needed to hold and comfort her. Before he took his first step, his father sat next to the girl.

His dad placed his hands on her wrists. "Alexandra," he gently asked, "can you describe how you are feeling?"

Alexandra lifted her head and took a deep breath. "I can hear you all talking to me. But it's almost as if you are coming in with all sorts of static. I don't know how else to describe it."

Just as she said those words, her nose started bleeding. Alexandra wiped her nose and then looked in horror at the blood that covered her hand.

"Oh my God! What is happening to me?" Alexandra cried.

He saw his father look at his mother, she then nodded and left the room.

"Alexandra," his father said, "you may have been born in another world, but your parents were telepathic. They would have passed on to you the same brain chemistry they had, but not the knowledge of how to use it. What you call static are the communal pathways trying to connect with your brain. Leenea is preparing a beverage full of herbs that will reduce the impact of the random chatter that is coming your way. We give the same herbs to our children, as they learn to manage the familial and communal pathways. The blood is a common side effect."

His mother came into the room carrying a steaming mug and a wet cloth. Tarsea saw Alex take the beverage from her and breathe in the scent of the herbs. Even without taking a first sip, he noticed her color was coming back. She wiped the lower portion of her face and her hand with the cloth.

"There are a variety of herbs I collected in your world," Darden shared with her, as Alexandra sipped the beverage. "They are contained in that drink."

She glanced at him and Tarsea continued to stare back at her. Alexandra sipped from the mug, not saying a word. From time to time she would inhale deeply and exhale slowly. More and more color was coming back into her cheeks.

His mother came back into the room carrying a small saucer. She said something to Alexandra that was so quiet, he could not hear. The girl placed the bloody cloth onto the saucer. Then her stomach let out a loud growl. She looked up, embarrassed.

Alex could feel her face redden in embarrassment after her stomach growled. Falling through a portal to another universe had interrupted her dinner plans. With everything happening, she finally realized she was hungry.

"I do not know about anybody else, but I am starving," a young man with curly black hair commented. "My name is Tolfer. I am Tarsea's younger and better looking brother."

Alex could not help but laugh. He looked to be about her age. She saw a definite family resemblance between the two brothers. Although Tolfer seemed more at ease, where Tarsea had to be one of the most uptight men she had ever encountered. Regardless, she was extremely attracted to Tarsea.

"I have prepared one of my world famous keen dishes," Tolfer continued. "It is about ready to be pulled out of the oven. Give me a couple of minutes, then we can eat dinner."

Tolfer left the room, as another man came up to her. "Hello, my name is Starc. I am Darden's twin brother. This is my cousin Koel." Starc nodded to the man standing next to him. Both men were almost as tall as Darden and as good looking.

Alex now knew everyone in the room. She took another sip of the herbal concoction. It smelled wonderful and tasted delicious, but she needed something more substantial in her empty stomach. The herbs did reduce the static in her head.

"Keen is a grain that grows in this world," Leenea shared with her.

"Is it purple?" was Alex's reply. She always used humor to defuse a stressful situation. She felt some of the tension in her stomach lessen. There was no question in her heart these people were doing everything they could to ease her into this new world.

"Yes," Koel answered, flashing her a silly grin. "You catch on fast."

She saw the family resemblance between Darden, his twin brother Starc, and their cousin Koel. All three had blond hair, the same nose, shades of blue eyes, and were tall. Darden's hair looked almost bleached, like a California surfer. His twin had more of a strawberry blond tint, while Koel had dark blond hair.

However, it was short black hair that kept catching her eye. She noticed that Tarsea kept staring at her throughout the whole discussion. Her eyes kept returning to his. He was making her uncomfortable. She needed to redirect her mind to something other than her fixation on the man.

"Darden," Alex inquired, "I still don't understand how you found me and Shirl."

"Eight years ago I was in Sedona," Darden replied. "I literally ran into Benko Jarlyn and his daughter. He had been keeping an eye on the four of you. Eventually he trusted me enough to share his secret about you girls."

"The four of us?" Alex frowned. "I thought it was just me and Shirl."

"No," Darden answered. "There are also Candace Phillips and JoAnna Carlson. If you include his daughter Cassie, that makes a total of five female offspring that Benko and his followers had. Shirl and JoAnna were actually born here in the Troyk Universe. They were carried as babies through the portal as your parents and their friends left this world for what they hoped was a new beginning."

"Oh my God! Candy is one of us too?"

It was actually starting to make sense to Alex. The games the girls played to freak out the care workers in the orphanage had to be related to their telepathic abilities they did not know they had.

"Wait," Alex continued. "JoAnna Carlson, do you mean Jo Jo?" It would explain how close the four girls had been and how difficult it was when Jo Jo was taken away. That event further solidified the girls' resolve to stay together.

"Frankly," Darden responded, "I do not know, Alexandra. She had been with you at the orphanage and was adopted before Benko could stop it. She is in Florida now, living with her adopted father."

Alex was thrilled that one day she would be reunited with her childhood friend. She worried that Jo Jo was experiencing the same headaches that were crippling Shirl.

"It would appear," Zane shared with the group, "we have a lot of work to do to bring the other four girls home and not draw unwanted attention. In the meantime, I agree with my son, I am hungry. Let us eat and then we can talk more on this matter." Zane got up from his perch near Alex and walked to a large table that had somehow been miraculously set.

Alex joined the group as they made their way to dinner. She had never really felt comfortable with others besides Shirl and Candy. For some reason, she could not explain, she felt a part of this close knit group of family and friends. There was a comfort level that made her ask questions and not feel self-conscious. For once she felt visible and a part of the whole.

Yet again, she turned and there he stood. It was almost as if he was a phantom, a shadow that could not be touched. As they settled around the table, she hoped Tarsea would sit next to her and they could talk. She was disappointed when he went to the opposite side of the table. Did she do something to repel him? He certainly stared at her enough.

⁓ᴑ

Tarsea felt like a coward. He could sense that Alexandra wanted him to sit next to her, but he was terrified they would accidentally touch. She shifted in her chair, obviously feeling anxious again. He could not imagine what she was going through. His little pixie was handling her new situation extremely well. The fear and apprehension he had seen earlier in her emerald eyes was gone. It was replaced with an adventurous gleam.

Tolfer came out with several dishes. His younger brother had turned out to be an excellent cook. His mother and father both conceded the preparation of meals to him when he was home. He loved both his parents, but neither could prepare food. Tarsea had always mooched off Darden's family for meals. Tolfer did not have a close friend and ended up learning out of desperation. Although Tolfer had his own apartment, he often came by and cooked for his parents. If Tolfer did not come over, his parents would go out to eat. Even they could not subject themselves to their own cooking.

As the dishes were passed, he noticed Alexandra take in the aroma of each dish and serve herself. She would take a cautious first bite and then had a look of pleasure on her face. After she tasted each dish, she dug in like she had not eaten in weeks. Tarsea was enchanted watching her and had not touched anything on his own plate, until his brother asked him what was wrong with the food.

"This deep purple dish is delicious," Alex said. "What is it?"

"That is the keen," Darden responded. "Many vegetables, grains, and proteins in your universe are also found here. Keen is unique to this world."

Darden had answered her, since he was the most familiar with the foods and beverages of her universe. Tarsea tried to figure out how he could join the conversation. He had never been lost for words before and started to get frustrated. Not only was Alexandra peering at him from time to time, but his parents were giving him questionable looks. He was surprised they were not cross examining him about his behavior using the familial link.

"You mentioned I had an aunt who lived in the next province. Is it safe to see her?"

Tarsea felt this was his opportunity to jump into the conversation. He also wanted to eliminate any concerns she may have regarding her safety. Earlier, he had telepathically asked Darden the same question.

"Your aunt had been a secret follower of Benko Jarlyn," Tarsea responded. "She attended many meetings with your father and mother before they left. We can eventually place you in her custody. However, we would like you to stay here for the time being. After the display of carrying you through the streets, we want to make sure you draw no one's interest before you travel outside this house. We also have to get you comfortable using the communal pathways. In the meantime, we can contact her and have her visit."

Alex smiled at Tarsea and it took his breath away, at just how gorgeous she was. A warm feeling spread through his body, as he basked in that smile of hers.

His mother and Tolfer got up to clear the table. Alexandra rose as well. "Please, let me help. That meal was wonderful." His mother smiled at her and she grabbed a couple of plates and followed her into the kitchen.

Tarsea had just gotten up as Alexandra was making her way back to the table to pick up more dirty dishes. She tripped on part of the rug that had curled over and started to fall. He reached out and caught her. As his skin made contact with her, he felt as if he had been electrocuted.

Chapter 6

Alex felt like every nerve ending in her body was on fire as Tarsea held her. He seemed to be as strongly impacted as she was, judging by the startled look in his eyes.

Tarsea righted Alex. "Are you all right?"

She took a deep breath, took an inventory of her burning nerve endings. "I think so," she responded. "Just embarrassed that I haven't learned to walk yet." She backed away from Tarsea, stepping away from the heat that he emitted.

"My pixie is so adorable when she is flustered."

Alex thought she heard Tarsea say something, but his lips were not moving. At this point her eyes were transfixed on his lips, his very kissable lips. She was losing her mind, which could explain why she was hearing voices.

"You can kiss my lips whenever your little heart desires, sweetheart."

Now that was not her imagination. Although his lips were not moving, his eyes gave away that he had somehow said those words to her. Was she having her first telepathic communication? No one else seemed to be reacting to what he was saying.

"Are you communicating through one of the communal pathways to me?" She continued to survey the room. No one seemed to hear what Tarsea telepathically shared with her.

"You really are a spitfire! The angrier you get, the cuter you are."

She had enough!

"This is not funny, Tarsea," Alex said. "Why are you saying all those personal things to me through a communal channel?" She liked what he was saying, but was embarrassed that everyone else in the community was privy to it.

Alex noticed the others were looking at her with a variety of expressions. Darden looked at first surprised and then intrigued. Tarsea's parents looked between Alex and their son with pure wonder. The others just looked confused.

"Leenea and I need to talk to our son and Alexandra in my study," Zane finally broke the silence. "If you boys will excuse us."

Alex followed them into the study. She needed to calm down so she could have a somewhat coherent discussion with Tarsea and his parents. Taking several deep breaths, she let each out slowly. She did a quick visualization exercise Shirl had showed her to clear and relax her mind. To her amazement, it actually worked.

"Well," Zane asked his son, "is she your soul mate?"

"Yes," Tarsea responded. "We had our first physical contact when I caught her, I felt the soul mate link open. I had suspected up on the mountain. I was afraid to touch her and find out I was mistaken."

"Good God!" Alex said. "What are you two talking about? I know what a soul mate is and you can't just touch someone and know if that is the case or not."

She knew she had a violent reaction to his touch, but there had to be another explanation. These people were telepathic, he was probably the first person she had picked up thoughts from. Soul mates, please!

Leenea took Alex's hand. Her touch calmed Alex. "As we told you, Alexandra, we have telepathic abilities. On rare occasions two people have the ability to open a telepathic channel that just the two of them share. It is activated with the first physical touch."

"*It is true, my little pixie,*" Tarsea once again channeled to her. "*We are soul mates. I have caught snippets of conversation from you, I am sure you did not mean to send to me. The channel we have been using is the soul mate channel. I am sure of it.*"

"Stop calling me a pixie! I know I am short and I hate when people call me pet names that are related to my size." Alex had always been sensitive about her height. She always felt dwarfed by her Amazon girlfriends, Shirl and Candy. Although she heard the rest of what he said about the soul mate channel, she did not respond to that part of the communication. She was still trying to deal with everything they were telling her about the special channel.

"Stop antagonizing her through the soul mate channel," Zane chided his son. "Talk to the girl. You are not making this any easier on her."

Tarsea straightened his posture and gazed at her. Alex never had a man look at her the way the man in front of her was, he seemed to be worshipping her. If worship was the right word. She was equal parts embarrassed and excited by his gaze.

"I am sorry, Alexandra. You cannot imagine what it means to me to have finally found you. Soul mates are things of legend. When you came hurtling through the portal, I knew you were my soul mate. I have been holding myself back. From the beginning, I have wanted to capture you in my arms. In my efforts to control myself, I guess the immature teenage boy I use to be came back to the surface."

Overwhelmed by what he had said, she re-examined everything she had felt for Tarsea from the first time she laid eyes on him. Alex had been lusting over this man from the start. It was also true, there was an unexplainable inherent trust regarding him. His words were the first telepathic communication she had heard. What was hard to swallow was they could communicate in a legendary channel between fabled soul mates.

"Listen, I do not know about this whole soul mates thing, or whatever you say we are. How do I know this is not just communication through a communal pathway? I've never experienced any of this telepathic stuff before."

Tarsea looked at her. He was probably used to women throwing themselves at him. The guy probably could not deal with anyone challenging or saying no to him.

She lost the game of chicken. She broke eye contact with him. He was forcing her to make the next move, she had no place to go.

"Assuming I believe you, how can I talk to you in your head? You also mentioned I leaked words to you. How do I stop doing that?"

The idea certainly intrigued her. She could imagine the conversations they'd have if what he was saying was the truth. She had heard of phone sex, but never personally experienced it. The thought of such a conversation with him started to raise her temperature, yet again. She hoped she was not turning all shades of red. He disturbed not only her body, but her mind as well.

"You need to concentrate on me," Tarsea told her. "Imagine pushing a thought in my direction. Look at me and do not think of anything but me. We do not want you to enter the communal pathway. The opposite is true related to not sending words or phrases in my direction. When you are thinking of me, try not to push those thoughts in my direction. It will take some practice. The soul mate channel appears to be very sensitive in what thoughts are picked up."

Alex focused her entire being on sending Tarsea her first thought. She wanted to make it as impersonal as possible, in case she entered one of the communal pathways by accident. She had no idea what he was talking about, but knew she needed to start trying and understanding telepathic communication.

The more he concentrated, the more the static started to increase in her head again. She felt blood dripping from her nose.

Tarsea waited to hear his soul mate's voice in his head. He watched Alexandra concentrate in order to use the soul mate channel. To his horror, he saw blood trickling from her nose.

His mother left the room, no doubt to get more herbs and a wet rag for Alexandra. Tarsea in the meantime, grabbed a couple of tissues and handed them to his soul mate.

She eyed him suspiciously as she accepted the tissues. Although he wanted to hold her, he got the non-verbal communication that she wanted him to keep his distance.

Alexandra started crying. It tore him apart. Disregarding her body language, he brought her into his arms. He drew her closer, lowering his head to take in the scent of her hair. Ironically, she smelled of a beautiful purple tinted flower, lavender. His soul mate molded to him beautifully. A feeling of contentment that was new to him brought a calmness. He took another deep breath and took her scent into his lungs. He was relieved she let him hold her.

"It will be all right," Tarsea said in a soothing voice. "It will take some time to learn how to manage the channels."

As he held his soul mate, it came to him that the feeling he was experiencing had been written all over his father's face when he saw his parents holding each other. He looked at his father and saw him in a new light.

"You are soul mates," Tarsea said. It was not a question, he somehow knew that was the case.

His mother re-entered the room as he stated what he knew was a fact. She stopped in her tracks, then continued toward his soul mate after recovering. He released Alexandra, as she took the mug with the herbs from his mother. Alex's eyes held his as she started to sip the herbal mixture.

Neither of his parents responded to his statement. He needed to discuss with them why they had hidden their relationship all these years. Most importantly, he wanted to know what it meant to be soul mates.

"You now know we are," his father replied. "The mind control telepathic movement was starting to gain momentum when I met your mother. We connected at one of the opposition underground rallies, since it was no longer safe to meet in public. Everyone was suspicious of each other. When we realized we were soul mates with the first touch, we decided to keep it quiet."

He watched as his soul mate continued to sip more of the herbal beverage. She had a hard time accepting what they were. The next question he needed to ask his father was guaranteed to further alarm her. He had no option, he had to ask regardless. Alexandra needed to understand everything involved in being a soul mate.

"Is it true about the evolutionary change that occurs with soul mates?"

"What?" that obviously caught Alexandra's attention. He watched as her gaze moved between him and each of his parents.

His mother obviously knew Alexandra was beginning to panic and took his soul mate's hand into hers. "When soul mates make love for the first time, a hormone is excreted from the brain. That hormone enhances the telepathic abilities our brains possess. There is no pain involved, not like what you are experiencing with the communal channels."

His father nodded in agreement with what his mother said. "All we have discovered to date is we have a natural immunity to mind control influences. We can enter a single mind to communicate, but not the ability to manipulate that individual. Your mother and I are careful when we do it. We make it appear to be a communal channel. That is how we have been able to rise in the government safely and aid in the rescue of dissidents before they are captured."

"If we do not wish to have a conversation," his mother added, "we can merely listen to someone's thoughts."

⌒𝓸

Tarsea seemed to take in stride what his parents were telling him. Alex on the other hand was freaking out. Although she had heard Tarsea in her mind a couple of times, she had not done anything telepathically on purpose. The idea of additional powers, or whatever it was, was not a welcoming thought. She did not want to think about her brain excreting anything. It was terrifying.

"Since Alexandra has not been using her telepathic abilities," Tarsea's father said, "any change would be just part of her normal experimentation of using new faculties. Tarsea, you will be able to navigate the different factions within the government and be better able to determine who you can trust and who you cannot."

Alexandra's energy started to wane. After all, she worked half a day, drove up to Sedona, traveled through a portal to a parallel universe, and met her supposed soul mate. The adrenaline rushes she had several times since coming to the Troyk Universe were used up.

"Can we sit, Tarsea, I'm exhausted."

"Alexandra," Tarsea said with wonder, "you just talked to me telepathically through the soul mate link!"

She was so tired, she had not realized she had sent those words telepathically. Whatever she did seemed so natural, it was done without thought. There had been no stress on her brain, no nose bleed.

Tarsea led Alex to a couch and they both sat. He put his arm around her and she cozied into his body. It felt right. She made no attempt to leave his side or distance herself from him.

"Alexandra is exhausted," Tarsea continued. "It has been quite a day for her. We can put her in my old bedroom and I will sleep in Tolfer's former room tonight."

Leenea stood. "I will make another mug of the herbs for Alexandra to help her sleep. It will help you continue to manage the communal pathways and allow you to relax and get some rest. I will be back in a couple of minutes."

Alex was too tired to tell Tarsea he should sleep in his own bed and she'd take his brother's room. Soul mates or not, she was also relieved that he did not want them to share a bed tonight. She was not ready to take the dive into those waters, including any evolutionary change.

Tarsea was sitting quietly next to her, he loosened his grip on her a little. She closed her eyes and worked to turn off the static building in her head. He smelled of herbal soap and of male. She loved his scent, taking in another heady breath.

Leenea came into the study with the steaming mug of herbs she promised. She handed it to Alex, as before Alex drew the aroma into her lungs with a cleansing breath. Tarsea's mother disappeared again as Alex took a sip of the herbal concoction.

Alex had just finished draining the mug as Leenea entered the room. "I have put fresh linen on the bed in Tarsea's old room and have found something for you to sleep in." Alex took the mug, rising from the couch.

"I will say good night to you here, otherwise, neither of us will get any sleep." Tarsea gave Alex a light and tender kiss. As kisses went, it was pretty damn sweet. *The next set of kisses will not be so sweet, Alexandra. They will be full of the passion I have been holding for you.*"

Alex followed Tarsea's mother to the bedroom. His words kept playing in her head. They both excited and terrified her. For once in her life she was reacting physically to a man. She seriously questioned whether she'd be able to manage this situation in her cool and controlling manner as she always did in the past. Alex felt she was close to combustion and wondered how she was going to handle Tarsea.

Chapter 7

~

Alex woke in a cocoon of soft sheets and what could have been a down comforter. She lazily stretched her body, not remembering the last time she was so comfortable. When she went to bed last night she was expecting to wake this morning disoriented, not knowing where she was. It was not every day you fell through a portal and found yourself in another universe.

Throughout the night she heard Tarsea quietly talking to her, making sure she was all right. She was not sure whether she answered him in reality or just in her dreams. Surprisingly, she was alert and knew exactly where she was. Alex was amazed that she was calm and thinking logically, even this early in her day. The heated sensations she felt last night had been mitigated due to her separation from Tarsea.

Although it pained her to leave such a luxurious bed, nature called. She had to face her second day in the Troyk Universe. Waking up each morning for Alex was always a challenge. She generally made her way to the shower in some kind of zombie state.

She stepped into the warm shower and the water pressure slowly invigorated her body. Leenea showed her around the bedroom and connecting bathroom last night. It amazed her how similar the shower was to the one she had at home, although it had a better showerhead. There was purple liquid in a bottle that she assumed was shampoo. She poured some into her hand and was overwhelmed with a floral scent. The shampoo lathered nicely and then she rinsed it out of her hair.

As Alex stepped out of the shower, she noticed the change of clothes Leenea left her last night. There was a light blue tunic and black leggings that ended up fitting her like a glove. Alex wondered where the outfit came from. Leenea had to be a good eight inches taller than she was. She slipped her feet into soft suede like shoes and was ready to face the day. Again, they fit her perfectly.

She followed the wonderful aroma into the kitchen. There was Tolfer cooking up a storm. His brother and the rest of the men were milling around watching Tolfer's artistry, as he put together breakfast.

Tarsea went to meet her and wrapped his arms around her. It felt so good to be in his arms. It continued to feel natural, which was weird since she had known him for only one day.

"Good morning," he said through the soul mate link. *"I hope I did not keep waking you last night. Each time I woke, I felt the need to check on your well-being."*

"I think you actually entered my dreams," Alex responded, *"rather than waking me up. I felt safe and secure while I slept."*

She did not know when she had been more brutally honest with anyone in her life. It felt instinctual to talk to him with such intimacy. Communicating to her soul mate Tarsea telepathically was now ingrained in her psyche. There was no strain on her brain, as there was with the communal pathways. She feared the communal path and another nose bleed. They said it was normal to bleed through the nose or ears when learning to leverage the various pathways. As far as Alex was concerned, it was foreign and gross.

Alex felt something must have leaked from her thoughts, since Tarsea let go of her. He poured steaming liquid from a tin kettle on the range into a mug. The scent of the herbal mixture engulfed the kitchen. Tarsea handed over the mug.

She let the aroma penetrate her lungs and then took a sip. Although she had been managing the static, she felt the pressure in her head weaken as she continued to drink.

"I am all done here," Tolfer said. "Let us all sit. We should talk about what steps we have to take today to blend Alexandra into Troyk society."

She appreciated that these men who usually communicated through their various telepathic paths were once again speaking aloud to include her in their conversations.

Everyone followed the platter of food into the common room and sat around the table. For one ridiculous moment she thought of the Pied Piper.

"Where are your parents?" she asked when she realized neither Zane nor Leenea were present.

"They have gone to pick up your aunt from the tram station." Tarsea shared with her between bites.

Alex choked on the food she had been chewing. She knew she was going to meet her aunt, but did not realize it would be so soon. One of her favorite dreams when she was little was having one of her blood relatives show up at the orphanage and taking Alex home with her. Shirl and Candy would come along as well. Her dream was now becoming a partial reality. She picked up a glass of water and started to sip the cool liquid.

She could feel Tarsea's stare. "To start off, we also thought Tolfer could work with you on how to use one of the communal pathways. You can listen in on what is being sent across the different channels. He teaches children how to manage the different channels they communicate through. Once we have your back story figured out, you can try to add something to that communication. Your head injury that we faked yesterday should buy us a day or two before people start questioning your silence."

She was not thrilled about linking into the communal pathway. Working with Tolfer made the prospect a little less scary.

"There is one change you have to make when you speak," Darden told her. "Here, we do not abbreviate speech with the use of contractions. You need to elongate your speech. You cannot, versus you can't. I have not, versus haven't. Got it?"

Alex had a sudden flashback to Freshman English. "Yes, I have it. This just gets more complicated. What else am I having to learn or change?"

"School is in session," Starc joined the conversation. "You are going to learn about the Troyk world. We can teach you about our government and your role in society."

This was the first time Starc had spoken directly to her since introducing himself, so what he said weighed even more in her mind. He was tall like his twin brother, but more muscular. His eyes were a richer blue, like the color of deep ocean water. They had to be fraternal twins, rather than identical. She had no idea if he was a crystal telepath like Darden.

Alex let out a long sigh, she never cared much for school. However, her education was more about ultimately earning a living, not surviving in a parallel universe. If Tolfer taught the way he cooked, she would be mastering the tele-pathic channels in record time.

"If that is not enough," Tarsea added, "the two of us need to get to know each other better."

That was definitely at the top of her list. She knew virtually nothing about this man who was supposedly her soul mate. Alex glanced at Tarsea and gave him what she hoped was an encouraging smile. Maybe if she knew him better, she would be more relaxed in his presence. Better able to handle the attraction she felt for him. It was not lost on her that every time he touched or held her, those fears and reservations disappeared.

"So, what is first on the agenda gentleman?" She pushed back her plate and was ready to dive head first into the choppy waters she was having to navigate in a short period of time. She was taken aback by how excited she really was to get to know about Tarsea and her new world.

"We all have places to be, so we thought you should have some time alone with Tarsea before your aunt arrives." Darden then faced the man in question. "We will all be back later this afternoon. You also have an appointment today that you need to handle as well."

Alex noted Tarsea gave her an uncomfortable look before he left to escort his brother and friends out.

Tarsea saw his friends and his brother to the door as Alexandra cleared the table. He saw the questioning look in her eyes when Darden mentioned the appointment he had later this afternoon. It would not have surprised him to have Alexandra leverage the soul mate telepathic channel and ask him about the appointment. He was now dealing with his soul mate and he made a pledge to himself right here and now he would not hide anything from her.

He made his way to the kitchen as Alexandra finished clearing the dishes. Tarsea liked how Troyk fashion looked on her. The tunic melded to her curves up top and the leggings brought out her shapely legs.

He wrapped her in his arms and whispered in her ear, "We should go to the couch, I need to talk to you." Although he could have used their channel, he liked the feel of being so close to her ear. He started nibbling on that delectable part of her anatomy and felt her immediate response to what he was doing.

Feeling ever so romantic, he lifted her into his arms and carried her into the common room. She weighed virtually nothing. He smiled, remembering one of his first thoughts on the mountain was about feeding her. He started thinking about all sorts of ways he would feed her. Let us see, in bed, naked, lips to lips and so on.

She giggled and nuzzled his neck. Once he reached the couch, he let her down. They both got comfortable, entwined together on the sofa cushions.

Alexandra broke the silence and finally asked the question he was waiting for. "What appointment do you have this afternoon? You had a look of terror on your face when Darden mentioned it." She looked so concerned, it warmed Tarsea's heart.

"Our government is run by the Prime Council and is ruled by a man named Jeryl Jarlyn. A faction that uses mind control is in power, a faction that my father and friends have been secretly fighting. We must appear to support this faction in the work we do that is visible to all and the relationships we have. One of the most powerful members of the council is Prime Adholm."

Tarsea took a deep breath, ready to share with Alexandra the piece of news he knew would not make her happy. "I have been dating his daughter Chartail."

"Dating," Alexandra asked, "as having slept with her?" He noted her stern expression, which did not surprise him.

Tarsea nodded. "Yes," Tarsea confessed, "we have slept together. She is a nice girl who I used for her connections. I knew it was never going to turn into a serious relationship, but my cover was critical to mine and others' safety. There was no question she was not my soul mate. Frankly, I did not believe soul mates existed until you came through the portal yesterday."

"Describe her to me," Alexandra demanded. She was not going to just let this go. He was kind of flattered by her jealousy.

Before he had the time to respond, she got within an inch of his face. "If she is tall and blond, you are in serious trouble." She was ferocious and as sexy as any woman he had ever encountered.

He pounced on her, pushing her back into the couch. Tarsea started kissing her lips with an urgency he had promised her last night their next kiss would possess. His right arm caressed the curves the tunic covered, while his left arm went down along her leggings. He continued to ravish her succulent lips while she wrapped her legs around his waist.

"She is tall and blond," Tarsea shared with her, *"but she never made my blood boil the way being with you does."* He knew she would ultimately meet Chartail, so the sooner he addressed the question, the better. Alexandra appeared to have issues with tall blondes. He continued to assault her body and he could hear little noises coming out of her.

"Tarsea," Alexandra pushed through the link, *"I have to come up for air."*

He backed off for a minute, while she caught her breath. He licked his lips, savoring her taste. She tasted of herbs and something uniquely Alexandra. The taste was addicting.

"Wow!" Alex sighed. "You are really good at this. As a stalling mechanism, that was commendable. Plus the kiss wasn't bad either." She took another breath, smiled and then it was her turn to go on the offensive.

A wave of cold water hit him and Alexandra when his father's voice broke into their lust filled conscious. "We made better time than we had expected and the shuttle was early."

Tarsea and Alexandra released each other in a split second and sprang to their feet almost simultaneously.

He looked at Alexandra, whose eyes were transfixed on the stranger who stood between his father and mother. The woman was of short stature, like his soul mate, and had her coloring. There was a strong family resemblance between the woman who stood next to him and the one across the room.

He heard a stifled cry from Alexandra. Tarsea watched her run across the room, to be met half way by her aunt. The two women embraced, both crying uncontrollably.

Alex held her aunt as if she was drowning and the woman was a piece of wood, keeping her from sinking into the dark depth of the ocean. She felt the dam of emotions break that every orphan experienced when they found out they were not alone in the world. Alex started to cry along with the woman who was shaking in her arms.

She did not know how long she and her aunt held each other. It appeared that neither woman wanted to break the embrace that was a lifetime in the making.

"Oh, my little Alexia," her aunt cried. "You are finally home."

Alex released her aunt, took a step back and wiped the tears from her face. "Alexia?" she asked her aunt.

"Your mother Starta must have named you Alexandra after our mother Alexia," her aunt explained.

Alex looked at her aunt. She had the same shade of green as Alex's eyes and her hair was a little lighter auburn with streaks of gray. Never in a million years had Alex ever believed she would find out why she was named Alexandra.

"My friends call me Alex," she shared, "that's pretty close to Alexia."

Her knees were shaking and she needed to sit. She took her aunt's hand and led her to the couch.

Leenea came in with a couple steaming mugs of the wonderful beverage that always made Alex feel better. She handed one to each of the women, while Zane gave his son another beverage and joined them. The men were probably drinking something stronger than herbal tea, Alex thought.

"They mentioned you were my aunt," Alex said. "I guess you were my mother's sister." She had so many questions she wanted to ask, but did not want to overwhelm the woman. It also dawned on her that she did not even know her aunt's name. "I now know what my mother's name was, but I don't know yours."

Her aunt smiled and shared with the group, "My name is Norri. I still cannot believe you are finally home. What happened to your mother and your father, Blaylot?"

Alex had not known her parents' names until today and truly felt their loss. She tried to hold back the tears that started to roll down her cheeks.

"They died before I even had any memories of them. I was born on Ear-- in the Ginkgo Terra Universe and I understand there is something in the air that attacks our telepathic brains when we reach our mid-twenties. Although I cannot know for sure, but I believe that killed them. I was told they died in a car accident."

Norri nodded her head. "I expect it was asking too much to get Starta back as well. She was my twin sister. We were so close when we were growing up."

Alex could see Norri was trying to come to grips with a loss that occurred so long ago, but a hope that had lived for so many years.

Alex concentrated on her aunt and attempted to push a thought to her. "*I know I cannot replace my mother, but you have me now.*" There was no additional static or nose bleed from her first attempt at using the familial link. She noticed her aunt's gaze fell back on her and a sad smile graced her face.

"Yes, I have you now. It has been a long time since someone used the familial pathway to communicate to me. My parents died ten years ago. I had no brothers or sisters, other than Starta. We have extended family somewhere, I had not bothered to maintain a relationship."

Alex did not want to take any chances after the telepathic push through the familial link. She took several large gulps of the herbal beverage. Hopefully, it would counteract any negative impact on her brain and she would not get a bloody nose.

"You are welcome to stay with us as long as you like," Leenea said to Norri. "You are part of our family now, although we will not be able to link into your familial channel."

Norri looked confused. "I thought the plan was for me to take Alexia home with me. After Darden contacted me originally I started mentioning a distant relative that would be moving in with me. I was surprised to hear from Darden so soon. I had thought it would be another year or so before he would bring her back."

Tarsea spoke up. "Fate intervened sooner than planned. Alexandra fell through a portal that Darden opened yesterday. We were all taken aback, especially when I found out she is my soul mate."

Tarsea moved closer to Alex. It appeared he was staking a claim and it amused her. She had found her aunt and her supposed soul mate. Alex hoped she would not have to choose between them any time soon.

Some of the tension Alex was feeling was relieved when her aunt smiled. "I figured that was the case when we walked in here and saw the two of you together. There was a magic about how you two fit together, almost like an energy emitted from you. Fortunately, my employer has their main office here in the Aster Province. They had been pressuring me to move here for years."

There was a commotion at the door as Darden, Koel, Starc, and Tolfer entered. Introductions were made and the four men joined the group. Alex noted how comfortable her aunt was with the men and started to actively participate in the conversation. It would appear her aunt had found a new extended family, one that welcomed her, as they welcomed Alex.

Leenea brought in more of her luscious beverage and the group came up with a cover story that would explain Alex's presence here, as well as her aunt's. Norri was considering taking her employer's offer to relocate to the Aster Province. Alex was a distant cousin who had lived with Norri and had come here to check out the area. In the process of hiking she fell and was found by Tarsea, as he was meeting up with Darden. They brought a hurt Alex to Tarsea's parents' where he started to fall for her. There would be no mention of being soul mates, but they could mention the strong first attraction that impacted them both as she started to recover from her fall.

Now that they had the cover story figured out, it was time for Alex to try and hook into one of the communal channels. Tolfer spent a little additional time with her, giving her pointers on navigating the channels. She concentrated on the static and caught one stream to focus on. It took several tries, as she just had the connection and then lost it. Her hand continued to find its way to her nose, making sure she was not bleeding.

Finally, she got a clear communication, *"Leenea, how is the girl doing"*…*"She is doing much better"*… Alex focused and pushed her thought into the conversation trail *"Thank you for your concern, I am feeling much better"*…*"Have the headaches gone away?"*…*"No, I am still suffering from them"*…*"Alexia, you should rest"*… Alex heard Zane enter the conversation and pulled out of the communal pathway.

It was a strange experience, but she felt comfortable that she could manage going in and out of the streams. She had the excuse of headaches caused by the fall that would allow her to go in from time to time and practice. All the mugs of the herbal beverage she had consumed must have worked. Alex did not feel any negative effect of her first trip into a communal pathway.

Later in the day, Tolfer made dinner and Norri volunteered to help. Turns out her aunt loved to cook and was excited to prepare a meal for such a large group. Alex knew as more time passed, Tarsea would have to leave to make his appointment. She could feel him getting more and more anxious. From his words earlier, he knew he was going to hurt the girl and was not looking forward to the task. Alex was not comfortable with Tarsea meeting with the woman, but there was nothing she could do about it.

She leaned over and gave him a sweet kiss, like the one he first shared with her. *"You have to go and see her. Do what you have to do. When you get back we can continue what we started before your parents showed up with my aunt. Come see me in your old bedroom, if we have all retired by the time you get back."*

She knew what she was offering Tarsea. For once she was attracted to a man and she had to trust her instincts and her body. She just wished she could trust Tarsea. He was going off to meet his gorgeous blonde girlfriend, leaving her behind.

Chapter 8

~

Alex leaned back on the sofa in the common room, sipping the herbal mixture that reduced the static in her brain. She had spent the last hour getting to know her aunt and working on her telepathic abilities. At one point she was able to leverage the familial link with Norri, joined in a conversation within one of the communal channels, and orally conversed with Leenea.

Norri was getting comfortable in the guest room that would temporarily serve as her room until she found a place near her employer's office. She was vacillating whether her aunt should get a one or a two bedroom apartment. There was a definite connection between Tarsea and herself, but she did not want to rush things. The fact that he was meeting with his girlfriend should have caused red flags and alarms to go off. For the time being, maybe she should live with her aunt. Perhaps they should get a three bedroom apartment to provide space when Shirl and Candy came.

There was a knock on the door and she heard Leenea go to see who had come to visit. She could hear voices and then footsteps coming toward the common room where she was perched.

"Alexia," Leenea announced, "this young man is here to see you."

In the cover story they created, her name was Alexia. It had been her grandmother's name and she was named after her. As she got familiar with people, she would start having them call her Alex.

Alex looked past Leenea and saw a tall, well-built man with sandy brown hair and light brown eyes. This universe was certainly full of good looking men!

The man came forward and extended his hand. "Hello," he said, "my name is Raine Narmouth. I was on the mountain yesterday when you were carried off it."

Alex had no idea who this man was, so she was going to play ignorant. That was going to be easy, since she had no idea what was going on. She had a hard time believing that Leenea left her alone with this unknown man.

"Thank you," she responded, "for any assistance you provided. I cannot believe that I fell when I was hiking. It was really embarrassing when I came to and found out what happened." The cover story seemed to be working. She was comfortable telling the story and it had a ring of truth about it. Alex also knew this type of conversation between strangers would be done orally, even in a telepathic world.

"Well," Raine continued, "I must have taken a spill myself, since I cannot remember the last three days. When I came to yesterday morning, I was on the mountain. I heard through the communal pathway that you had been there as well. Did you see anything?"

"I must have been taken off the mountain before you had your spill. Neither Tarsea nor Darden said anything about anyone else being there when they brought me down. I do not remember seeing anyone as I was making my way up the trail either."

"Interesting," Raine responded, "I was told I was dispatched to the mountain because a second mass came through the portal shortly after Darden exited."

Alex did not know what to say. She remembered being warned that a patrol would be coming because of a second body coming through the portal.

"I am not sure what happened. Tarsea met Darden at the portal, and shortly thereafter heard my scream as I fell. Did Darden explain what the second mass was?"

"Yes," Raine replied, "he said a rabbit was dragged into the portal before it closed."

"Wow!" Alex exclaimed, "Your sensors can pick up something as small as a rabbit?" She wanted to kick herself for saying that out loud. Darden would not have reported something that could not have happened.

Raine Narmouth stared at Alex for a moment and then started laughing. "The sensors are sometimes so sensitive, they can pick up a butterfly. Most of our trips to the portal are a waste of time. I keep telling them they should adjust their sensors to detect a mass big enough to create a threat."

"How would you be able to determine the mass was a person versus a large animal?" Alex probably should not be so interested in the intricacies of the portal, but she was fascinated. After all, they still had Shirl, Candy, and Jo Jo to bring through. Her new friends also had hopes that Benko Jarlyn and his daughter would also be returning to this world.

"We would not be able to differentiate between a man and an animal. A physical inspection has to be performed. An animal could be just as dangerous as an unknown person coming through the portal. We once had a giant larma beast come in from Terra Flora. He was a challenge to catch and place in the Aster Province Zoo."

"Wow, I would love to see it at the zoo!" Yet again the words were out of her mouth before she judged whether they should be uttered. Between oral communication and the communal pathways, she knew she needed to take better care of what she said.

"I would love to take you, Alexia."

Alex swallowed, boy, did she just mess up. Did he just ask her out on a date? Was she obligated to go with him? What was she going to tell Tarsea?

Raine must have sensed her discomfort. "I know you are still recovering. How about when you are feeling better, in a couple of days we will go. The zoo has animals from a number of different worlds and is quite a sight to see."

She really wanted to check out that zoo. Her soul mate was on a date, after all. It would be natural for someone from another province to go out with a couple of men when she first arrived. Raine was also very good looking.

"I would like that, Raine." Alex knew she sounded genuine because she really wanted to check out what animals from other worlds looked like. Deep down inside, she knew she wanted to see those animals with Tarsea by her side.

"How about we go three days from now? We can have lunch at the zoo. They actually have a charming restaurant within the park."

"Sounds great!" It really did. In her former world, it would have been a perfect first date.

Alex got up and escorted Raine to the door. He looked at her and then walked out the door. For a second, she was afraid he was going to kiss her.

She closed the door and turned to see Leenea. Her stomach sank when she saw Tarsea's mother. Why did she feel like she had just stolen a cookie from the cookie jar and was caught red handed?

"I could not help but ease drop," Leenea said. "You handled that very well. I would have come to the rescue if you had faltered." Relief eased the knot in her stomach. Leenea had not abandoned her and she approved how Alex had managed the situation.

"You are not mad I made a date with Raine? After all, I am supposedly your son's soul mate."

"Before I married Zane, I dated many men, even though I knew Zane was my soul mate. It is all about keeping up appearances. However, there were probably better choices related to who you date. You just need to be on guard about what you say around him. He is a patrol officer, after all. It will all work out fine, wait and see."

"Yeah, I just have to convince your son of that." Somehow she knew Tarsea was not going to be happy about her going on a date with Raine Narmouth.

Chapter 9

~

Tarsea arrived early, so he could have a drink before his meeting with Chartail. His time now with Chartail could be called many things, but not a date. He ordered a stoak, distilled keen, on the rocks. The liquor burned on its way down, a warmth spread through his body. Alexandra caused a different kind of heat to rush through his core. He longed to have her next to him and taste her lips. He knew they had a lifetime ahead of them. He needed to finish things with Chartail before he could take the next step with Alexandra.

The crowd began to grow and the music became louder. He felt the bass line in his bones and ordered another shot. Tarsea grabbed some salted crisps that were in bowls along the bar and popped them into his mouth. He started to scan the bar for Chartail. She always wore bright colors and stood out in a crowd. That was what first attracted him to her. Now that he had met Alexandra, he knew what real attraction meant.

A bright yellow flash on his left caught his eye. Chartail was wearing a bright yellow transparent blouse with a short cream colored skirt. She rarely wore the tunic and leggings that most of the Aster Province's population wore. He made his way through the crowd and embraced her.

Chartail smiled at him and placed a kiss on his lips. One more action he was going to have to confess to Alexandra when he saw her tonight. Tarsea took her arm and shouted over the noise in the bar. "How about us taking a walk. It is too loud in here." He led her to the exit adjacent to the park.

There were half a dozen paths available in each of the meeting place's parks. Tarsea decided to take the longest one, since it would be close to abandoned this time of day. He wanted to have as much privacy as possible when he talked to Chartail.

She started the conversation before he had a chance to speak. "I heard you found a hiker on the mountain who had fallen when you went to meet Darden yesterday."

Tarsea was thankful she had brought up how he met Alexandra. This would be a perfect lead into what he needed to tell her. The communal pathways were more aware of Alexandra than he originally thought.

"Yes," he responded, "Darden had just come through the portal when we heard a woman scream further up the path. She was unconscious when we found her. The girl had no identification on her. We decided to take her to my parents' house and see how badly she was injured. Having woken in the hospital bed after a fall myself years ago, I know how frightening that can be." He knew he provided the cover story they created almost word for word.

"That was very sweet of you. I am sure the girl appreciated it when she came to and had your parents to look after her."

Chartail was usually clingy and tonight was no exception. Tarsea gently pulled away from her and readied himself to start the speech he had been rehearsing in his head for some time. He knew he would break up with her before things got too serious. Alexandra's presence just pushed up the timetable and nuances of what he was going to say.

"When we got to my parents, we placed her in my old bedroom," Tarsea continued. "She was placed in the bed I slept in most of my life. Chartail, I sat next to her and held her hand, waiting for her to open her eyes. I know you do not want to hear this, but I felt a connection to her before she even woke." Tarsea knew that part of the story was fabricated, but he stayed as close to the truth as possible, so it would ring true to Chartail.

"Wow!" Chartail exclaimed. "That was really slick! You sounded so sincere, Tarsea. We have been seeing each other for seven months now and I have been waiting for you to break up with me for the past few months. I knew of your reputation, that your relationships last three to six months and then you move on to your next conquest.

"I even tried to convince myself that you loved me, that things would be different with us. Who was I fooling? I do not know who I feel sorrier for, me or that poor girl." He knew she was angry, but he noted not a single tear fell from her incensed eyes.

"Chartail," Tarsea said, "you knew how I was before we started dating. I was not looking for a long term relationship."

Tarsea had to set the foundation, so Chartail would not be too surprised when he started to be seen in public with Alexandra. He could not afford too many questions or attention from her father Prime Adholm.

"I spent most of last night talking to Alexia." Surprisingly, that was actually true. He used Alexandra's Troyk grandmother's name, rather than calling her by her Terra Ginkgo name.

"Let me guess," Chartail said in a facetious voice, "you are about to say that you still want to be friends."

"We were never friends," Tarsea responded. "We were lovers, big difference." Not Tarsea's finest hour in his own opinion, but it had to be said. "I liked spending time with you outside of bed, but the bulk of our relationship was sexual. Maybe if we started as friends, this could have developed into something else."

"So," Chartail said, "am I being replaced by a newer model? Is she younger, blonder and slimmer? I know your type, you bastard! I was actually friends with three of your former girlfriends. They stopped talking to me when I started dating you."

"She is nothing like my type, Chartail. Maybe that is why I feel different where she is concerned."

Tarsea knew he had to paint Alexandra in such a manner that Chartail would not be threatened by her going forward. Because of her father, she was well connected socially. He did not want Alexandra to be a social pariah from the start.

"She is really short. I have always dated blondes, she has light auburn hair. A redhead, can you believe that?"

He wanted to sound like a besotted fool. Odds were he did, because that was exactly what he was.

Tarsea could tell that he had whetted Chartail's curiosity about Alexandra. Hopefully she and his former girlfriends would see her as the one who finally brought him to his knees and made him suffer in the process. His primary concern was Alexandra's welfare. For once he was driven by someone else's agenda, when it came to the relationship he was in.

"Looks like you have finally found someone who will throw you off your game. Good, I am dying to meet her and buy her a drink." She started walking in the direction they had come. "I am going back to the bar to see if I can salvage the rest of the evening. I really do hope she breaks your heart."

With those parting words, she increased the speed in which she walked away. Tarsea followed her at a respectable distance to make sure she got back safely.

"I am heading home, Alexandra. I will be with you soon." He did not know if the soul mate channel was strong enough at this point to cover the distance. It felt good transmitting to her, even if she did not receive it. He was ready to start the next part of his life with Alexandra. Now, he just had to convince her. He knew she had a lot of reservations about their relationship. Tarsea also knew that all he had to do was touch her and her body's needs took over.

Chapter 10

~

Alex heard Tarsea communicating he was on his way home. She smiled and laid back in his bed. Norri had spent the evening with her, telling stories about Starta and Alex's father Blaylot. Her aunt shared 3D images of her parents and grandparents. There were pictures of Norri and her mother growing up, often dressed in the same outfits. Things weren't so different here, compared to home where dressing twins was concerned.

Then of course there was the visit from Raine Narmouth. She was not sure how she was going to tell Tarsea about him and the date she had set up. Before, she barely had one boyfriend. She never had to deal with juggling more than one like other girls.

The house was so quiet that she heard when Tarsea returned. She patiently waited for him. Alex had hoped he planned to take her up on the offer she made him before he took off to meet with Chartail. She planned to erase his former girlfriend's touch from his memory, replacing it with hers.

Tarsea opened the door, came into the room and then closed the door behind him. He took a step toward her and then turned around to lock the door. She could not help but smile at the action. The last thing either of them wanted was for anyone to walk in on them again. That was so embarrassing this afternoon, what a way to meet her aunt!

As he moved forward, he slowly took off his tunic. Alex stared at his incredible chest. Tarsea was all muscle and sinew, he could be an underwear model. There was little hair on his chest, just around his nipples. He had more hair that started around his belly and disappeared into his leggings. She licked her dry lips, as he came closer.

He sat on the side of the bed facing Alex. The bed shifted as she moved closer to him. She took one hand and placed it around his back and used her other hand to explore his magnificent chest. There was nothing soft about Tarsea. He was built solid and she appreciated every inch of him. She had to taste him, she leaned forward and licked his chest. She made her way up and then started to nuzzle his neck. All of this was new to her. Never had she reacted to a man the way she reacted to him.

Tarsea gently pushed her into the mattress and came down to cover her body. He reached for her face and brought it up to his, so he could kiss her lips. Alex got lost in his incredible caress. His tongue invaded her mouth and possessed her being. She could not put two thoughts together, as he continued to deepen the kiss and explore her mouth with his skillful tongue.

Alex felt him adjust his position and he started to pull the lightweight tunic she wore to bed over her head. She raised her upper torso to help him remove the material that prevented them touching skin to skin. Before she could feel self-conscious about the size of her small breasts, Tarsea had his mouth on one and his hand massaging the other. He sucked and pulled on the hardened nipple. She was doing everything in her power not to scream in ecstasy. God that felt so good. Alex had been with other men, but never felt the rush of sensations she was feeling now. It had always felt awkward before.

Tarsea muttered something and moved to her other breast. He assaulted that breast as he did the other. The hand that had been working on her breast earlier was moving down her side and going into the sleep shorts she was wearing. He invaded the panties and worked a finger into her tender folds. Before she could cry out loud, his mouth left her breast and covered her mouth with a scorching kiss. A second finger entered her and they both worked their magic. He had a rhythm going and she was lost in the primal mating dance his fingers were performing. The fire was burning inside her, ready to explode as he increased the tempo. His mouth captured her scream as she fractured into the first orgasm of her life. She never thought she would experience the height of passion. The reality of it was more than she imagined possible.

"Are you all right, Alexandra? I was getting a lot of words from you through the soul mate link, but I could not seem to stop what I was doing." His words pulled her out of her sensual fog. Her brain had been overwhelmed by his touch and what he had just done to her.

Tarsea rolled off her and pulled her into his arms as he lay on his side. She rubbed her nose across his wet chest and took her tongue to yet again taste him. He tasted so good, she could not get enough of him. Salty goodness!

"I didn't know I was transmitting anything. I was kind of lost in the sensations you were bringing out in me." She managed to mutter those words as she continued to savor his taste.

"Your body was very responsive to what I was doing, but your mind started throwing off a lot of static when my fingers were bringing you what I hoped was pleasure."

Oh my god, he was talking about what he had done to her. She was caught between embarrassment and elation. There was an intimacy about the words, she had problems dealing with mentally. Alex knew she had to find words to describe how she was feeling, so he could not take random words ricocheting out of her brain the wrong way.

"I am fine, Tarsea. My mind and my body are not always in sync when it comes to men. You are the first man I have met who seems to get a reaction from both. It's usually just my mind reacting and my body staying neutral. Well, my body certainly reacted tonight to you and what you were doing. My brain must just be in a state of shock that my body has finally responded to a man."

"We are a telepathic people, Alex. I have to listen to your mind, as well as your body. I do not want to go any further until your mind comes to grips with what we are doing."

"How about we take a shower, while my mind is dealing with all these emotions and sensations?" Alex whispered the proposition in his ear. Her body was still craving every powerful inch of him.

Tarsea laughed and brought her closer to him. It felt good and natural to be next to him in bed. She had known him for only two days, but it felt like she had known him her whole life.

"I think you need a good night's sleep and we will talk about showers, as well as brain and mind harmony tomorrow. You worked your brain hard today, experimenting with all the different channels. I could feel its fatigue along with the static. When we are finally together, I want it to be an experience your body and your mind can cherish."

She could not argue with what he was saying, although she wished she could. As much as she tried, she could not reign in her brain and the experience she just had with him.

"I won't pretend to be disappointed, but I understand what you are saying." Alex snuggled next to Tarsea. "Just don't go yet. Why don't you keep holding me and tell me how things went this evening."

He brought her further into his body and tightened his hold, she liked being this close to him. As he spoke, he made little designs on her back with his fingers. She figured he did not even know he was doing it.

"She was naturally upset. I do not have the best track record with women and long term relationships. Chartail said she was expecting me to break up with her, but reality is a killer when it actually happens. I described you to her and she said she hopes you break my heart. Oh, she also said she will buy you a drink when she meets you."

"Time to come clean," Alex said, "how did you describe me?" She was dying to know.

"Well," Tarsea laughed, "I actually told her the truth. That you are a fiery redheaded pixie who is always making demands. For once in my life I got to know a woman rather than jumping into bed with her."

"She bought that?" Alex asked. "We've only known each other two days." Although they had talked, she wondered what they just did. It certainly felt like jumping into bed to her.

"Alexandra, you are my soul mate!"

"So you keep telling me. But the world doesn't and shouldn't know. Your mother told me they dated other people to keep up appearances for a while." She could feel his body tighten next to her.

"You talked to my mother about this?" Alex almost laughed at the look of horror that crossed Tarsea's face. Alex swallowed hard, the moment of truth had come. It was time to fess up.

"Yes," she said sheepishly. "We talked about it after I accepted a date from another man." Alex knew she ripped the metaphysical Band-Aid off the topic. Tarsea growled yesterday, she was half expecting him to howl tonight.

"You what?" Tarsea released his grip on her and sat up. He took a dominant position over her and glared.

"Raine Narmouth came over this afternoon to ask me about yesterday and the experience on the mountain. He took a spill as well and could not remember. The guy stopped by to see if I was there and could shed some light on what happened." Alex wanted to sound as a matter of fact as she could. She did not want to project the same anger that Tarsea was emitting.

"That son of a bitch! You actually accepted a date with that bastard?"

Tarsea got up and started pacing. He appeared to have a lot of aggression he needed to walk off. Alex decided she needed to keep playing defense, he was really upset. She could not figure out if it was the fact she had a date or who she had the date with.

"Tarsea," Alex began, "you need to calm down and look at the big picture. The world cannot know we are soul mates. I am new in town and a nice looking guy asks me out on a date. Under normal circumstances, one would expect me to accept. After you and I have dated a while, we can become exclusive and I will stop dating other men."

"You are not going out on a date with that man, Alexandra! That is the end of this discussion. It is too dangerous." He was now almost standing over her, his arms crossed over his chest.

"Yes, I am, Tarsea, and that is the true end of this discussion." Accepting a date with Raine was probably not the smartest thing she could have done. However, Alex had it with Tarsea's dictatorial manner. She was furious he was telling her who she could and could not date.

Tarsea gave her a lethal look and stormed out of the bedroom.

Well crap, that did not go well, Alex thought as she punched the pillow that Tarsea had used earlier. How was she going to fix this and still maintain as equal a position in this relationship as possible? On top of everything else, she was now committed to going on a date, she really did not want to go on.

Chapter 11

There are morning people who can get up immediately and dive right into their day. They do not have the morning haze of grogginess that clouds their minds. Tarsea had always been a morning person. He never saw the appeal of lounging in bed. That was true, until this morning, when he woke up with Alexandra in his arms.

When he had sex with a woman he would leave after they were done, and headed back to his apartment. He never brought a woman to his own bed. There was something too intimate about bringing his latest girlfriend to his home. His dating served a purpose, he never felt any of them were real relationships. That all changed with Alexandra. He could never imagine ever going to bed again without his little pixie right next to him. His world changed forever this morning, with her entangled within his embrace.

He regretted the argument they had last night. She actually made sense once he cooled down. He had come back in the room after she had fallen asleep. She should be seen with other men. However, he could not stomach the idea of her spending time with that worm, Raine Narmouth. The man was untrustworthy and he did not want Alex near him. If she needed to be seen with other men, she could start with Starc or Koel. These were men he could trust.

He stared at the woman he held in his arms. Although she was so small, she fit perfectly against his body. Her face was as delicate as the rest of her. He gently held that small chin of hers that she lifted in defiance when she thought she was being tough, just like last night during the argument. Turning her head ever so slightly, he brought her small mouth with full kissable lips closer to his own. He further lowered his head, giving her a welcoming kiss to her day, as she started to wake up. His soul mate was not a morning person that much was clear to him.

Alexandra moved restlessly next to him and moaned in denial that morning had arrived. He knew she was going to wake slowly and he was going to orchestrate it. Tarsea decided to continue his exploration of her face. He made his way up to her nose and gave it a short loving kiss, then kissed both her closed eyes. Her ears and neck were calling to him to provide the same morning discovery, he found himself engrossed in. Tarsea then attacked her ears and Alexandra's breathing increased. She stretched out her neck to give him better access and let out a different kind of moan. As Tarsea started to kiss and lick her neck, Alexandra began to rub his back with her hands.

"Good morning," she pushed through their channel. *"You came back to bed! Don't stop what you are doing on my account."* Tarsea smiled and continued to explore Alex's body with his lips. He savored her taste with every flick of his tongue. His hands at this point had been content with just holding his soul mate.

He continued his journey down her neck and started to pay attention once again to her perky little breasts. *"I was so absorbed in loving your breasts last night, I did not have a chance to tell you how perfect they are."*

Tarsea had caught telepathically a little concern from her the previous evening that he would find these perfect mounds lacking. It had not been a true communication, but he had picked up a fragment of a thought. He needed to assure her that he loved every part of her body, especially these beauties.

Taking one nipple into his mouth, he sucked and his tongue played with the taut nipple. One of his hands was playing with the other nipple, gently squeezing and massaging the skin around it. *"Tarsea, you are driving me insane. I don't know how much more of this I can take."* He smiled as he worked to build up her insanity and continued to make her putty in his hands.

He was just about to start working on her other breast when he started to hear unexpected chatter in the communal link. It stopped him cold and he sat up. Multiple channels had communication coming through that provided sketchy information that something was happening at the Aster Province Palace.

Alex sat up next to him drawing his attention. *"There is so much static in the communal links all of a sudden. It's too much to manage."* She was holding her head in her hands.

Tarsea rubbed her back with one hand, trying to soothe her. With his other hand, he lifted her face from her hands and looked into her eyes. *"You are doing the right thing. Keep concentrating on the soul mate link and communicate with me. We should get dressed. My mother will have some of the herbal beverage for you to help with the activity that is hitting the channel."*

Tarsea gave her a quick kiss and left their bed. He grabbed his tunic from the floor, pulled it over his head and made his way to the common room.

His parents were already up, talking to Alexandra's aunt Norri. There was concern written on everyone's face.

"Does anyone know what is happening at The Palace?" Tarsea asked. "There is a lot of chatter occurring on a number of the communal links."

Tarsea spoke aloud so Norri could be brought into the conversation. At this point the only link she had access to was through Alexandra.

"One of the opposing factions took some kind of action this morning," his father shared with him. "It is unclear who is involved or what exactly happened."

Tarsea and his father looked up, as his brother and Koel came through the front door.

⤳

Alex almost immediately missed Tarsea's presence in their bed. She found it funny that she was already considering the bed they slept in last night as their bed.

The static in her head was getting louder. She decided to take his advice and leveraged the soul mate link. *"Were you able to find out any more about what is happening?"*

"Tolfer and Koel just arrived. There is still no definite news about who was involved or where things stand. Darden and Starc are still outside The Palace trying to find out what has occurred." Concentrating on what Tarsea was communicating did help to defuse the chatter coming through the communal channels. It was still a strange sensation, hearing voices in her head.

Alexandra stretched and decided she should join everyone in the common room. She tumbled out of bed and did her typical morning routine in their bathroom. Rather than having a toothbrush, the Troyk used a liquid they swished in their mouths and then spit out. It somehow was the equivalent of brushing. She did not know if it was as effective as brushing and flossing, but her mouth felt refreshed every time she used it.

She put on a beautiful lavender and gray tunic, along with black leggings. This morning she decided to put her hair up. Last night she had asked Leenea for hair pins and was rewarded with all sorts of cool accessories. She had confessed to Alex that she always wanted a daughter, and before they met up with her aunt, she had stopped by a store and purchased a number of items that could be used with her light auburn hair.

She could once again feel liquid coming out of her nose. "Shit!"

Alex grabbed a couple of tissues. These nose bleeds were still plaguing her and she was getting frustrated that she could not properly control the channels! Fortunately, none of the blood dripped onto the tunic. She conversed with Tarsea about nonsense through their private channel, which helped reduce the chatter assaulting her brain. Once the bleeding stopped, she made her way to the common room. She had snagged a couple of tissues on the way out, just in case. She stuffed them in her tunic's sleeve.

As usual, she was greeted by Leenea carrying a steaming mug of the herbal remedy. Alex graciously took it from the lovely woman who she grew to love more each day. She sat next to Tarsea and started to sip the miracle brew.

Tarsea had a baked good in front of him and she began to snack on the remainder of what was on the plate. It was made of a berry she had never eaten before and it was delicious.

"Anything new?" she inquired from Tarsea through their link. She, at the same time, greeted her aunt by projecting through the familial link, *"It's wonderful to see you this morning, Norri."* In addition, she greeted the others in the room who she did not share a closed pathway with, "Good morning." Alex was quite proud of herself, she had managed two parallel transmissions and verbal communication all at the same time and no new nose bleed. After popping another piece of the berry muffin into her mouth, she sat back and was ready to receive telepathic and oral responses.

Tarsea smiled and gave her a chaste morning kiss in front of their respective families. *"You are a fast learner. Remind me of that tonight when we are in bed."*

The mischievous smile he had on his face disappeared and the scowl that she knew so well from the mountain returned.

"We know a faction tried to assassinate Jeryl Jarlyn this morning. He was on his way to address the Prime Council when the attempt was made. At this point, that is all we know." Tarsea was back to being all business.

"That is correct," Koel continued the update. "We know two of the palace guards were killed in the attempt. Jarlyn was not hurt, but he is out for blood."

Koel rubbed his left temple and got up to get a drink. Alex was relieved that she was not the only one having problems dealing with all the activity occurring in the communal channels.

Tolfer came in from the kitchen carrying a tray of food and placed it on the table near Alex. "Starc and Darden are still outside The Palace and are keeping us updated through our special link."

Alex reached for more food, took a couple of bites and then turned to Tarsea. "You have a special link with your friends?" She once again spoke aloud, since her aunt could be as clueless as she was.

"A couple of years ago," Tarsea shared with the group, "a closed link developed between Darden and myself. We had no idea why the two of us could share thoughts that were protected from other channels. Over time Koel, Starc, and finally Tolfer were able to link in."

"That is rather odd," Norri said. "I never heard of a closed communal link connecting five friends."

Norri looked at Alex and walked a small box to her. "This is for you. It was your mother's." She handed the gift to her.

Alex took the treasure and held it in her hands. She took a deep breath as she lifted the top from the box. Inside was a copper bracelet, like the bracelets worn by everyone else in the room. "Each family has their own set of designs on their clan bracelets that celebrate the history of their ancestors. Your mother left the bracelet in my care when she left this world with your father." Norri helped Alex with the clasp.

She stared at the piece of jewelry on her left wrist, a bracelet that her mother had worn. Tears she could not control started falling down her cheeks. Tarsea pulled her into his arms and kissed her head. Emotions caught up with her. *"I don't know why I'm crying, I'm such a girl!"*

"Thank the Supreme Being you are a girl, you are my girl. The bracelet is part of your history, a history you knew nothing about. You are truly home now, my little pixie."

As the morning continued, there was no new information coming forward regarding the attempt on Jeryl Jarlyn's life. The communal channel was full of speculation, but little fact. Tarsea continued to hold Alexandra, participate in meaningless conversations and tried not to have his anxiety spill over to his soul mate.

Tolfer continued to work with Alexandra on managing the communal pathways. She appeared to become more and more confident going in and out of the channels. The chatter in the pathways reduced somewhat, since no updated news was available. He had also noticed she required less and less of the herbal mixture his mother kept preparing for her. He had never been prouder of his brother. This is the first time he was able to witness his brother's skills in teaching.

It was approaching midday when Darden and Starc entered the house. All attention was directed to the two men and the information they would share.

Darden was the first to speak. "Prime Hosp and several unidentified men tried to break into the Jarlyn's quarters through the servant's entrance this morning. Whatever intelligence they had was either bad or someone in their group turned informant. The guards were waiting for them as they entered the living quarters. Unfortunately, two of the guards were killed before it was all over."

Tarsea could not believe Prime Hosp had been involved in the plot. The man seemed to embrace a peaceful transition away from mind control telepathic rule. Obviously, he had been involved in other plots that Tarsea had no knowledge of. Like Tarsea, he must have gotten frustrated with how slow change was occurring. Unlike Tarsea, Hosp took steps for a radical change that involved violence. Ill planned and executed, change would not come from this attempt. It would also retard the progress that peaceful groups were trying to bring about.

"The first two men who entered the quarters were greeted with kill shots to their brains." Starc continued where Darden left off. "Prime Hosp and what was possibly two other men were trapped in the stairwell. One of the men must have gotten away, but before he did, he bashed Prime Hosp's skull in."

"Why would he do that?" Alexandra asked. "I thought the man supported the Prime and his cause."

Tarsea could only speculate. "He must have felt his chance of succeeding was next to impossible at one point and needed to eliminate the one person who could tie him to the attempt."

Darden nodded, "Prime Hosp is still alive. But even if he survives, he will not be sharing information anytime soon. Another man was found dead at the stairwell entrance to the kitchen. Doubtful if he was the man who attacked Prime Hosp. He had no blood on him or a weapon that could have been used against the Prime. The person who quieted Hosp did a real number on him, he would be covered in blood."

"They have shut down The Palace and everyone who tries to leave is being interrogated before they are allowed to go. A fellow gatherer was nice enough to fill us in after he was cleared to leave The Palace." Darden gave Tarsea a knowing look. "Jarlyn will be meeting with his staff in a couple of hours, after an initial examination of the bodies and other evidence is completed. Odds are they will be collecting names of Hosp's associates and start further investigations after that meeting."

His father got up. "Tarsea, I want to talk to you alone in my study, now!"

He did not bother to argue with his father, but followed him. *"I will be back shortly,"* he shared with Alexandra.

As soon as he closed the door to the study, his father lost no time in starting the conversation that brought both men there.

"It is just a matter of time before you are called to The Palace. Take that girl into your room and have sex with her, if you have not already."

Tarsea was momentarily stunned by what his father just said. "Do not look so shocked! She is your soul mate. Once you have sex with her, you will be able to counteract any mind control technique used against you at The Palace."

"That girl is my soul mate, I am not going to rape her!"

His father got a sour look on his face. "Who said anything about rape? You two were all over each other yesterday and cannot be in the same room together without touching. Your mother and I are going to take Norri out to dinner. We decided to give poor Tolfer the night off. The house will be all yours this evening."

"There is no question she is ready physically for us to be together, but her mind is not ready. I felt it last night. I am not going to rush things and have our first time together be for ulterior motives." Tarsea could not believe he was having this conversation with his father.

"You are an idiot!" his father pounded his fist on the desk. "Do you think for one minute you are the only one who will be brought in for questioning? Alexandra was paraded through the streets for all to see, two days before the attempt on Jarlyn's life. There is no question she is going to be questioned about her presence here. That time table was just moved up, due to the assassination attempt."

Tarsea could feel the blood rushing to his head and sat. "I was so focused on the attack at The Palace, I had not thought about the questions we were preparing Alexandra for the last few days. The coming together of soul mates should not be done in this manner. It just is not right. I wanted it to be beautiful for her." He was crushed he could not make it special for Alexandra. However, he understood the necessity to rush things along.

His father sat next to his son and put his arm over his shoulder. "That is one tough cookie you have there. She is up for what life throws at her. Alexandra will just lift that stubborn chin of hers and trudge forward."

It was with those words, the woman they were talking about stormed into the den. She stood in front of Tarsea, ready to breathe fire. "You come with me now, no arguments," his soul mate demanded. Before he could open his mouth, she was on her way out of the study. She continued walking, but turned her head and shouted, "Now!"

On his way out of the room, he turned and looked at his father. He had an amused look on his face. "Good luck," he called as Tarsea left the study and followed Alexandra into his bedroom. He was going to need every bit of luck he could get.

His soul mate looked ready to kill.

Alex marched toward their bedroom, she was so angry, she could spit. The shouting match between Tarsea and his father was heard by everyone in the common room. She had never been more embarrassed in her life. Everyone had pretended not to hear what was going on in the other room. Alex had to break up the fight and settle things with Tarsea.

Entering the bedroom, she sat on the bed and awaited Tarsea, who was right behind her. He closed the door and stood against it. There was uncertainty written all over his face, his body language did not reflect the confident man she was accustomed to seeing. For some reason, he looked defeated. Alex's anger seeped away.

"I'm going to talk aloud so there will be no misinterpreting anything I am feeling." Alex needed to get across to him how she felt and knew she was going to have to open parts of herself she had hidden from everyone her whole life. "I have been invisible most of my life. My two true friends are beautiful and confident, while I blend into the background. The orphanage did not encourage individualism and I just stayed back and supported anything Shirl and Candy wanted to do. In school I could not find anything that excited me. I work in a call center, one of hundreds of employees, working in a nondescript cubicle. What few relationships I have been involved in have been nothing special. Girls my age dated, so I dated."

Tarsea moved toward her and Alex lifted up her hand to stop him. "Every man I meet I fantasize about, that he'll be the one to break the nothingness I feel inside. My brain was going a mile a minute, but my body is still frigid. Then I fell through the portal and saw you and every nerve ending I possess started to burn."

Alex got up and started to walk toward Tarsea. She directed him to the bed and pushed him down, so that he was the one now sitting. "You make me burn, Tarsea, but this relationship can't be directed only by you. I need to be part of every decision made. I won't be pushed to the background where we are concerned. That discussion with your father should have been with the two of us. It is our decision whether or not we are going to make love in order to start the evolutionary change that could save us."

She took a step back and slipped out of her shoes. In the best shimmy she could do, she removed her leggings. "I should have said something last night, when you stopped making love to me because for some reason you thought I wasn't ready to take the next step." Alex then slowly brought the tunic up her chest and then over her head. "The thing is, you cannot make the decisions unilaterally anymore. We have to do that together." She then slipped out of her panties and the material that bound her breasts.

She stood nude before him. For the first time in her life, she was confident in her body and in herself.

"There is a strong attraction between us and a strong practical reason to go forward as well. So, do you want to make love to me now?" She did not wait for an answer, she grabbed the ends of his tunic and pulled it over his head. She then sat and straddled his hips, pressing her lips against his neck and started to suck. She continued to lick, suck, and bite as Tarsea lowered them onto the bed.

She could feel Tarsea shifting to remove his pants, as Alex started to attack his ears. His short hair gave her greater access and she was going to take advantage. Alex was going to taste every square inch of him. She felt his hand on her hips as he flipped her onto her back, taking control from her.

"I want to taste you again," Tarsea transmitted to her before his mouth attacked her lips. She opened for him and his tongue dove into her mouth.

Alex ran her hands over his shoulder blades and down his back. She loved the feeling of his taut muscles, there was not an ounce of fat on his magnificent body. He released her lips and moved down her body to take one of her breasts into his mouth. She was all for an encore of last night's performance.

He sucked harder, to the point where ecstasy was on the verge of pain. She could feel him back off with that thought. She really needed to learn how to control what thoughts she transmitted to him. *"Oh no, you don't! Keep doing what you were doing. Don't you dare back off because you think I feel a certain way! I will tell you if I don't like something or if you are hurting me."* Tarsea went back to sucking harder and she loved it. Her breathing became labored and she arched her back even more. She released a breath when he switched his attention to her other breast.

His hand made its way to the juncture between her legs and entered her with one finger. She let out a moan. Oh God, that felt good. *"More and faster,"* she pleaded with Tarsea and he once again did her bidding. A second finger joined the first and he continued to work his magic. Tension within her body continued to build until she had the second orgasm in the last two days.

Tarsea removed his fingers and moved up her body, once again capturing her mouth. Alex pounded her fists on his back and demanded, "Flip over! It's my turn to take control." She felt confident and ready to consummate this relationship. Wait a minute, she thought, consummate, she had been reading too many historical romance novels about virgin brides. Her mind was ripped from that ridiculous thought as he flipped them and she could feel the cool air on her back.

Alex pushed her now wet hair out of her face and gazed at the man looking at her with utter wonder. She bent down and kissed him like her life was dependent on it. She knew she should say something to him, but she could not figure out what. It was too early to say she loved him, she felt something, and Alex was just not sure it was love. There was certainly a lot of lust involved!

Lifting her mouth from his, she adjusted her position, straddling him and grabbed his fully aroused member and slowly impaled herself on his shaft. She went slowly, inch by lovely inch of him. He moaned as she brought him into her body.

"Alexandra, you are killing me," he managed to say. Tarsea yet again flipped them and he drove himself into her fully. She screamed, half surprised and half in amazement. He pumped in and out of her, increasing the momentum gradually.

"Oh, God! Faster, faster," Alex exclaimed. As instructed, Tarsea increased the speed and she was keeping pace with his thrusts. Yet again, she felt the friction building and wanted to hold off as long as she could so they could climax together. She milked him and she knew he was close, oh so close. Then they both fractured together.

As they both let go, she felt something in her head sizzle. She did not know how else to describe it. Tarsea collapsed on top of her, holding her tight. He was still inside her and she tightened her legs around him to keep him there. She still felt odd, but having him deep inside her made her feel better.

The strange feeling in her head continued and she could not ignore it any longer. "Tarsea, something is happening to me. My head feels strange, I can't explain how, but it does." The euphoria of their lovemaking was waning and Alex started to have a mini panic attack. "Something is wrong!"

"It is all right, relax. Your brain is excreting a hormone. This happens when soul mates make love the first time." Tarsea pushed strands of hair out of her face and looked

into her eyes. "The same change is happening to me as well. I have to admit, I had forgotten about this part while we were making love."

This whole time, a part of her did not believe in all the nonsense she was being told about soul mates. The fact that she felt the hormone excretion proved what she had been told was true. Tarsea was truly her soul mate. It was her turn to look at him in wonder.

"So, we are going through this evolutionary change? This will protect us against mind control? When does it stop? Are the effects immediate?" Alex had a zillion and a half questions, but she also knew she had to get herself under control. She took a deep breath, closed her eyes and concentrated on Tarsea's body next to her. His arms encased her, she wore him like a coat. Her breasts were smashed against his chest. She could hear his heartbeat. Her heart started to beat in sync with his. His staff was still inside her, she could feel it come back to life. She moved her pelvis and then moved it again.

Tarsea moaned and raised up on his forearms and looked down at her, smiling. "You little minx! Since all decisions are to be made together, I assume you want to go another round."

"God, yes," Alex answered him. He growled and started moving back and forth again. Tarsea increased the speed with each thrust, just as she liked it. She appreciated how Tarsea adjusted how he made love to her, taking her feelings into account.

"Are our brains going to do that funny thing again?" Alex asked breathlessly as she kept pace with his thrusts. It had not hurt, but she was still freaked out about her brain excreting anything. Obviously, the desire for sex again trumped any true concern. She decided to stop worrying about it and concentrate on making love to Tarsea.

They climaxed for the second time before he answered her. "It only happens once. I am not sure how quickly we are going to feel the change, though." He kissed her lips and withdrew from her body. "I think we should take a shower and then grab something to eat. If we are lucky, there are leftovers from one of the dishes that Tolfer made. Can you cook?"

"If you are half as good in the shower, as you are in bed, cooking can become my second passion." Tarsea got a gleam in his eye, collected Alex and carried her to the shower.

Chapter 12

The house was quiet. It did not reflect the changes and energy that had occurred in it over the last several days. He had met and made love to his soul mate. Tarsea's life had changed, but the kitchen where he sat was as it had always been. He was not really sure what he had been expecting, but not normalcy.

Alexandra walked into the kitchen. Her hair was still wet from the shower. She was all in black and had eye makeup on. *"Are we going somewhere, why the make-up?"*

His soul mate smiled. *"If I am going to be brought in for questioning, I want to look good."* Although she hid her anxiety with a smile, he knew she was worried about being brought before Troyk officials or even Jeryl Jarlyn himself. *"Besides, I wanted to look good for you."*

"You always look great," Tarsea said. *"Even when you are falling through portals in those ridiculous boots of yours."* He knew he would get a rise out of her whenever her diminutive size was mentioned. His little pixie was adorable when she got her dander up.

"Those boots were very expensive and are very stylish," Alexandra replied. "Besides, they were a birthday present to myself. I'm starving! I owe you a meal after that performance in the shower." He was memorized by the smile that graced her face as she said those last words. It was somewhere in between saucy and innocent.

She started going through the cabinets, pulling out different items and examining them. When she got to the spices, she would open each bottle and sniff its contents. Some of the spices were placed back in the cabinet and others were kept out. He loved to watch the variety of faces she made as she reacted to the scent of any given herb. She went into the cold storage area and pulled out a few more items. "Is this chicken?"

He looked at the package she presented and he nodded. She proceeded to unwrap the chicken and wash the pieces as she pulled them out. A bowl was taken out of the cabinet, as well as several pans. Alexandra started humming while she cooked, and it fascinated him. Time passed as he was transfixed watching her. Her black tunic was covered with the remnants of the spices she had used. The aroma of the dishes she was making pulled him out of his daze and his mouth started watering.

"So," Tarsea said, "we have a birthday to celebrate. How old are you anyway?"

"Twenty one," Alexandra said with a smile. "I'm officially a grown-up. How about you set the table."

He got up and started to do as she had instructed. In addition to the dishes he placed on the table, he brought out two wine glasses. From cold storage he grabbed a bottle of white wine and poured two glasses, handing one to Alexandra. She started to sip the wine while she put the finishing touches on their dinner.

They sat at the large table in the common room, next to each other. She watched him intently as he took a bite of the first meal she prepared. Flavor exploded in his mouth, it was delicious. The chicken was succulent and the side dishes were superb.

"I think I'll keep you," he communicated, while he continued to shovel the meal into his mouth. Alexandra smiled at him and started on her own plate.

Tarsea was on his second helping when the front door opened and a crowd entered the house. The solitude he had with his soul mate had come to an end for the time being. His father, Tolfer, and their friends went straight to the kitchen and helped themselves to a plate of Alexandra's creations. It was a good thing she had made enough for an army.

"I thought you went to dinner," he shouted at them.

"We did," his father said, "but this smells too good to pass up."

Tarsea watched as his father came into the common room, sat down, and ate a bite full of the meal Alexandra prepared for him. He saw his dad's appreciation of the dish written all over his face.

"Tolfer," his father mumbled with a mouth full of food, "you have some competition. Alexandra, this is wonderful."

"Thank the Supreme Being," Tolfer replied, as he joined them. His brother sampled the food and he saw his eyebrows rise in respect for her culinary talents.

The last of his friends sat with their own plates teeming with food. They quickly devoured Alexandra's efforts. All three mumbled various comments as the food on their plates disappeared.

Koel had just come back from getting what little was left of Alexandra's food when Leenea, Alexandra's aunt, and Koel's sister Tarah came into the house.

Tarah generally did not spend time with them, so her presence surprised Tarsea. He looked at Koel and transmitted through their closed link, *"What is your sister doing here?"*

She was a mind control telepath and he was not sure where her allegiances stood. Although Koel was always clowning around, he was serious about the fact they could trust his sister.

Between bites Koel said, "Tarah is going to question you. We will see if you both are able to protect yourself against mind control." He turned and faced Alexandra. "This is excellent, sweetheart. How about leaving Tarsea for me."

"Sorry, Koel, you are too much of a goof." She leaned over and kissed Tarsea on the cheek. "Besides, I kind of like the big guy here."

"If the legend is true," Tarah said, "I should not be able to tell if you are lying to me. Everything you say will be read as the truth."

Once again, he glanced over at Koel, who shrugged. Was there anything he did not tell his sister? Tarsea then looked at the blond woman before him. Tarah was thirty-two years old and he had little contact with her over the years, particularly when they were growing up. Koel had not started hanging around him and Darden until they were teenagers and Tarah was already at school.

He had nothing to lose. "We will give it a try," he communicated to Tarah.

Tarah sat back and glared at Tarsea. "Tell me how you were involved in the latest assassination attempt on Jeryl Jarlyn, instigated by Prime Hosp."

Tarsea looked at her in surprise. "I was not involved in this or any attempt on Jarlyn's life. Prime Hosp sponsored some of the bills that my father and I supported. I met with him on several occasions to discuss that legislation." As he talked, he could feel her pull on his brain. He was able to answer the question with half-truths, so she would not have been able to determine anything anyway. Mind control telepathic powers could only detect outright lies.

A mind control telepath could pull out falsehoods and direct someone to take an action that was not contrary to their base beliefs. Someone could not be compelled to kill, if they were not already predisposed to kill that person. The telepath could also not get someone to confess to a crime they did not commit. They could be compelled to vote a certain way or buy groceries at a certain store. As long as any doubt existed, the mind control telepath would be able to influence a decision. Choices people in other worlds took for granted.

"Do you know where Benko Jarlyn is?" Tarah fired back at Tarsea just as he finished his sentence.

"I do not have a clue where Benko Jarlyn is. He left when I was six years old. I never even met the man." As Tarsea communicated orally to Tarah, he leveraged their closed link to scold Koel. *"You told her about Benko Jarlyn being in the Ginkgo Terra universe? Are you insane?"*

"She can be trusted, Tarsea. I would stake my life on it." Koel responded through their closed link. He was showing a serious side, he rarely exhibited.

"Alexandra," Tarah turned to his soul mate and said, "where are you from and why are you in here?"

"My name is actually Alexia, but my friends call me Alex. My aunt is thinking about moving here from the Starling Province, so I decided to check things out for myself." Alexandra's response was natural. Tarsea was confident if she reacted to questions like this tomorrow, the interview would go smoothly.

Just as Alexandra finished, there was a loud knocking on the door. Tarsea knew their time was up and he could feel his pulse increase. He got up to answer the door. The first impression he made would stay with the men that came to get him. A confident man would be viewed as an innocent man. He opened the door and there were four soldiers standing on the other side.

The man standing closest to him presented his credentials. "Tarsea Childers you are summoned to The Palace to answer questions in regards to the attempt made this morning on our Prime Ruler Jeryl Jarlyn's life. You will come with us immediately. In addition, these two men have been instructed to bring your visitor, Alexia Montiff, for a private audience first thing tomorrow morning. They will stay outside this house for her protection this evening."

Tarsea turned to say goodbye to Alexandra and his parents, but was stopped by one of the guards. "You are to come with us immediately."

"It's all right. Tarah said she could not tell if we were lying or telling the truth. If you get home before I leave for my interview tomorrow, you better wake me up and make love to me."

He could not think of better words to leave the house with. Tarsea turned to leave and face the inquisition ahead of him. The guards posted were a sign that Alexandra's fate was tied to his.

Chapter 13

The Palace was humming with activity when Tarsea arrived. Evenings were generally a slow time, unless there was a governmental dinner or function. Every light was on, making the night seem almost like day. Soldiers marched in formation, fully armed. There was no question The Palace was on high alert.

He was led to the third floor, where the provincial governmental offices were. The guard he was following opened the door labeled 'Conference Room B.' He motioned for Tarsea to enter and then closed the door behind him.

There were three people sitting around the table, he knew them all. In the middle sat Harpath Holflur, who was in charge of the palace guard. He gestured for Tarsea to sit directly across from him. To his right was Solfa Theffar, who ran intelligence for the government. To his left was Prime Adholm, Chartail's father. He was in deep shit! He greeted all three members of the panel. As far as he knew, Prime Adholm was the only mind control telepath in the room.

Harpath Holflur started things off by setting the foundation of what they would be discussing. "I am sure you are aware of what transpired this morning, the attempt on Jeryl Jarlyn's life. Can you tell us where you were at eight this morning?"

Tarsea squirmed in his seat and looked over at Prime Adholm. "Well, I was in bed with a woman. Out of respect sir, it was not your daughter." This was either going to work out great or he was in real trouble. It was possible that the only mind control telepath in this room would be more concerned about his rejected daughter, than the attempt on the Prime Ruler's life.

The Prime Representative turned in his direction with anger written all over his face. "Yes, my daughter told me you broke up with her yesterday evening. I find it appalling that the evening you call things off with my lovely daughter, you are having sex with another woman. I also understand that it was in your parent's home. Do you have any morals what so ever?"

Tarsea thought he would take the offensive and make note that this was not about him, but Jarlyn. He needed to keep antagonizing Adholm so the other two would end this interview as a waste of time. There had been no pull on his brain, as there had been with Tarah.

"I thought this was about the attempt on our leader's life, not my complicated love life." Tarsea tried to sound offended, he hoped he got it right.

Solfa Theffar took over the questioning. She looked bored and a little aggravated. "Did you have any knowledge ahead of time about the assassination attempt?"

He was getting a strange vibe off her and focused his attention on what could possibly be a channel of some kind. *"This is such a waste of time. He may be a male whore, but he has always appeared loyal."* Tarsea tried to hide his surprise that he was able to read her thoughts. It must be another evolutionary enhancement mating with Alexandra had brought about. He remembered his mother had mentioned she was able to read people's minds.

Tarsea needed to answer her verbal question, instead of focusing on the communication that just occurred. "No, I was unaware of the attempt. I was shocked when I heard it was Prime Hosp. He always seemed to support the government. That was the impression I got from him."

It was at this point he could feel the mind control pull from Prime Adholm. He did not know if he was supposed to do something special, so he just reacted the way he did with Tarah.

"Are you aware of any other factions that may wish to do our leader harm or overthrow our government?" Harpath asked, as it appeared to be his turn to ask a question.

"No, sir," Tarsea replied. "I am not a political animal. My father and I have become wealthier under Jeryl's leadership. Any other person in power may not be as business minded. Best to stay with a winner then take a chance on an unknown entity." Everything he said was true. However, his success would have been more rewarding if people chose to do business with his family.

Prime Adholm leaned back in his chair, hooking his folded hands behind his head. "What are your feelings about using mind control to obtain a certain result?"

Tarsea knew this could be tricky, so he needed to navigate this one carefully. "As I said before, my family has become wealthier under this government. We pay our workers well, we pay our taxes and our society benefits. If mind control is responsible for that or can further improve our situation, I am all for it."

Chartail's father looked like he had the wind taken out of his sails. Obviously, the man could not pick up on the fact he had been lying. Tarsea felt this would be the end of the interview. That feeling was reinforced as Prime Adholm stormed out of the room.

Solfa Theffar laughed as the room echoed the slamming of the door. "You did not make any friends when you broke up with his daughter. A prudent man would not have even started up with that spoiled girl."

Tarsea returned her laughter. "I do not always think with my brain, unfortunately." Better to be thought of as a man whore than an instigator. Solfa gave Tarsea a long critical look.

Harpath Holflur gathered his papers and left the room. Tarsea was now alone with Solfa Theffar.

"You would have potential if you applied yourself." Tarsea tried to hide his shock when Solfa's thought came through the closed link. Her earlier thought had come from his mind reading capability. Never had someone outside his circle of friends entered the link he shared with them and Tolfer. It made no sense whatsoever.

"We all have to live up to our potential in the days to come," Tarsea said through the closed communication link. She could believe they were communicating in one of the many communal channels that were shared throughout the province.

Solfa looked shocked, she was probably trying to figure out which channel he communicated within. He needed to ascertain why she was able to get into what he believed was a closed channel.

"If this interview is over," Tarsea inquired, "am I free to go?"

Solfa still looked shaken, but answered his question. "Yes, Mr. Childers, you can leave. I am sure we will see more of you in the future. Good luck with the new girlfriend."

Tarsea got up to leave and nodded to her. Solfa once again used their closed link as he made his way out of the room. *"Jarlyn is only interested in her to see if she is his soul mate. It is his way to be introduced to every young woman entering Troyk society."*

Tarsea walked out of the room, as if that last exchange had not taken place. He was unsure if they were being watched from another room. He could now head home and planned to wake up Alexandra as he had been instructed to do.

After he made love to his soul mate, he needed to find out why Solfa was able to join his closed link. Something was not right.

Chapter 14

The streets of the Aster Province were deserted. Tarsea loved to walk at night. He took a deep breath of the cool, crisp air. There was little activity through the communal pathways at this hour. Fortunately, only conscious thought could be pushed through. Any thoughts that occurred in the dream state were not transferable. There was one person, however, he would love to find out what she dreamed. Getting into his little soul mate's brain would be quite an experience.

She really spoke her mind last night, as she seduced him. He had a feeling Alexandra held herself back most of her life. A little spitfire was starting to appear from the cautious girl who came through the portal. He could not wait to continue to see her transform before his very eyes.

About four blocks from the house, Darden joined him. He had risked using their closed pathway one more time before he left The Palace to have his best friend join him.

"We need to stop using the closed pathway for the time being," Tarsea said. "It has been compromised. Solfa Theffar entered it during my interview about Prime Hosp."

"Interesting," Darden replied. "I was expecting something like this would happen. Would you agree that our pathway feels like a hybrid between a familial link and a communal pathway?"

Tarsea gave his friend a surprised look, what an odd question. "Yes, but what has that got to do with Solfa entering our closed channel. I do not understand why you would have expected anyone else to join the link."

"I will explain everything later," Darden told him. "You can still use the link if we need to. It has not been compromised. We are getting closer to your parent's house. I do not believe we want the guards to see us together at this late hour. Get everyone together tomorrow and I will share what the link really is."

Darden left without another word. Tarsea did not know what game his friend was playing, but he would have to deal with it later. For now, he needed to concentrate on Alexandra.

He fumbled for his keys as he reached his parent's house. His mother had left the outside light on, her hope that he would make it home in one piece this evening. The light was certainly not for the two men who stood outside their home, waiting to take Alexandra to The Palace tomorrow morning. He acknowledged both men and entered the house. His presence should be words enough for them at this point to confirm his innocence. With his name being cleared, Alexandra's interview should be exactly what Solfa said it would be.

It was not surprising to see his mother and father were still up, awaiting his return. "Any trouble?" his father asked as Tarsea stood outside the entrance to the common room. He was always direct and to the point. It was a quality he admired in his father. The man liked to see the hand everyone was dealt before he decided on any strategies.

"Everything is fine. There has been an interesting development I will share with you in the morning. Nothing to worry about, I just want to join Alexandra." He did not wait for any response from either parent, making his way to be with his soul mate.

Tarsea was not surprised to find her pacing on the far side of the room as he entered their bedroom. She stopped dead in her tracks when she saw him, then pivoted and ran to him. Alexandra launched into his arms and started to kiss his face. She smelled of lavender and home.

"I was so afraid," she managed to say between the barrage of kisses. He backed her up, directing her toward the bed. Determining she was wearing too many clothes, he made quick work of removing everything she had on. She eagerly assisted him in the venture, then attacked the clothing he was wearing.

He drove her into the mattress, capturing her mouth. *"I told them I had to make it home tonight. I had an appointment with a little pixie who was going to make love to me."* She took a little nip of his lower lip in retaliation for the name that had become an endearment to him.

After the evening he had, he did not waste any time. He slid right into her with one massive thrust. There was an urgency in how he was feeling, a need to dominate. *"Where is the fire, big boy? Slow down, I can't keep up with you,"* Alexandra chided him. She was gasping for breath.

Feeling like an adolescent that could not control his lustful nature, Tarsea brought down the tempo so that she could play along. She adjusted the positioning of her legs she had wrapped around him, which drove him deeper into her core. They both let out a moan at the same time and Alexandra let out a little giggle.

He continued the pace she seemed comfortable with. His urgency gave way to her need to feel every nuance of the experience. They became one, her heartbeat matched his, beat for beat. He exhaled, she inhaled, their lungs falling in sync as well. Tarsea had never experienced anything like what was happening to them.

They climaxed at the same time, sharing their orgasm, as they shared everything else. He never experienced the syncing of a sexual release he had with Alex before in his life. As always, Tarsea brought Alexandra into his arms and held her as if he was never going to release her. Those men who guarded the house this evening were going to have to pry her out of his embrace.

Alex felt secure in her lover's arms. She preferred to think of him now as her lover, not her soul mate. It was too soon to say or feel that she was in love with him, but they were certainly lovers. There was more to what they did than having sex. She'd had sex, she knew the difference. She could also not deny that her brain excreted the hormone after the first time they made love. It was just another example of her mind trying to catch up with what her body was feeling and what was happening to it.

"Tell me what happened tonight," she asked as he played with a strand of her hair. She wondered what it was about men's fascination with hair.

"Three people interviewed me, including Chartail's father."

That certainly got Alex's attention. "You've got to be kidding! He must have been out for blood." If she was drifting off to sleep, that definitely woke her up.

"The man was certainly not happy. However, it worked to my advantage. The other two felt that the interview was personal. It was more about my relationship with his daughter, not about the assassination plot. The interview was over almost as soon as it began."

Alex could feel there was more to what happened tonight than Chartail's father being part of the interview. She felt he was holding something back.

"What else happened?"

Tarsea looked at her with such intensity. He seemed to be considering whether he was going to share something with her.

"Out with it!" Alex said. "Whatever you are debating whether to tell me or not, I am going to find out anyway. Frankly, you can save yourself a lot of pain and suffering at my hands if you tell me now." Alex lifted herself up on her elbow and glared at him.

"Someone breached our closed telepathic channel tonight," Tarsea confessed. "It was one of the interviewers. Her name is Solfa Theffar and she runs intelligence for Jeryl Jarlyn."

Alex frowned, that made no sense. "You sure you have not been dealing with a communal pathway the whole time? There are so many channels, who knows how they are created and leveraged the first time."

"This is different," Tarsea said, shaking his head. "Our pathway takes priority over both the communal and familial channels. It is clearer and we can negate chatter from the other links if we so desire."

"Wow!" Alex said in wonder. "How do I get linked in? That sounds wonderful. I love the herbal beverage and all, but it must be great to be able to shut everything out."

A thought came to Alex as she was considering the advantages of Tarsea's channel.

"The soul mate link," Alex considered, "it was able to drown out the intensity of chatter in the communal link. You said it was a channel of legend. Are there any other legendary channels that your closed link could be?"

She could see Tarsea was considering her question. He got a shocked look on his face all of a sudden.

"What?" Alex inquired. He looked like he had just found the cure for the common cold.

"There is another legendary link that is closed to only a few Troyk. Darden said he was expecting others to link in and he would tell us what was going on tomorrow."

"What channel are you talking about? Remember, I am not from around here. I do not know all the legends you grew up hearing." She had grown up with Cinderella, Sleeping Beauty and all those fairy tales. In this world, it appears legends were based on fact.

"The warrior link." Tarsea looked at Alex in wonder. "It is a link that supposedly the true leader of the Troyk shares with his or her most trusted staff and guard. The ability to link into the channel is proof to the true leader that the person is trustworthy and loyal."

"Darden has been the only one of you who has met with Benko Jarlyn. You said the link was originally between you and Darden. What if it really started between Benko and Darden?"

"I was thinking the same thing," Tarsea confessed. She had never seen such excitement in her lover's eyes.

Alex considered all they had just discussed and shook her head. "I have yet another secret not to reveal when I meet with Jeryl Jarlyn tomorrow. It wasn't as if I did not already have a mountain of secrets to deal with."

Chapter 15

Alex woke with a start. She had slept like the dead after Tarsea made love to her last night and they had their enlightening discussion. She had never met Benko Jarlyn, even though he had been keeping track of Alex her whole life. Looking at the hope in Tarsea's eyes at the prospect of Benko returning home and challenging his father for control of this world was awe inspiring. Rather than dreading her interview with Jeryl Jarlyn, she was actually looking forward to it. This was the man who drove his son and her parents to another world. She could finally put a face to the man she would become an advocate for overthrowing.

Today was not a day she had the luxury of lounging in bed. Tarsea's side of the bed was cold. Frowning, she got up and made her way to the shower. He should have gotten her up when he rose this morning. Clothes were laid out for her in their washroom. There was a long light lilac tunic and very sheer legging the same color.

She showered quickly and then put on the clothing he had chosen for her. The tunic clung to her like a second skin. What was the man thinking? She took a couple of extra moments to apply makeup that would be appropriate with the outfit.

Alex made her way to the kitchen. Various breakfast goodies were on display. She pulled out three mugs and three plates. She poured coffee into two of the mugs and the herbal beverage in the third. On the plates she selected a number of the pastries and muffins that were available. Placing the two mugs of coffee and two of the plates on a small tray, she made her way to the front door. Maneuvering the tray, she opened the door and walked out to greet the two men still guarding the residence.

"Here you go, gentlemen," she said, as she provided them coffee and breakfast. "Would you mind if I had some breakfast before we headed on out?"

The two men's expressions changed from surprised to appreciative in a matter of seconds. They took the tray she had brought for them. "Thank you, miss. We can leave in thirty minutes if that would be acceptable to you."

She did not miss the head to toe perusal the man who spoke gave her body. Men usually did that to Shirl or Candy, never to Alex. It was a new experience, one she was not sure she liked.

"That would be perfect. Enjoy your breakfast and I will be back shortly." She turned to go back into the house, only to see Tarsea standing in the doorway watching her.

She walked past him. Alex decided to put an extra wiggle in her walk, as Tarsea followed her. The heat of his stare was scorching. A little punishment for not waking her up this morning was called for. Grabbing the mug and dish she had prepared for herself, Alex walked in the dining room and sat to eat. Zane and Leenea were already at the table, finishing their coffee.

"What was that about?" Tarsea growled. She knew he was jealous and acted like a wounded animal.

Alex took a sip of her herbal beverage, then took a bite of the pastry she had selected. She was careful not to get crumbs on her clothing.

"You picked out this outfit, what did you expect? Besides, there is an old adage from where I come from: 'you catch more flies with honey than vinegar.' It does no harm being kind to those men. If I appear nervous and anxious, whoever interviews me will think I have something to hide." She popped the remainder of the danish into her mouth.

"Smart girl," Zane said with a smile, "you can learn from your soul mate, son." He leaned forward and grabbed the carafe on the table, and poured himself more coffee.

"Where is Norri this morning?" She noticed her aunt was not present.

"Tolfer took her out to breakfast and then house hunting this morning," Leenea shared with her.

"I was just telling my parents about the interview from last night," Tarsea said.

"Did you include Solfa linking into your closed channel and what you think it really was?" Alex asked.

"Yes," Tarsea replied, "we were putting a lot of subtext around what this could all mean." She really wished that Tarsea had gotten her up, so she could have listened and participated in the discussion.

Alex polished off her second danish and wiped her mouth with her napkin. She got up from the table, adjusting her tunic. "I better get going and get this over with."

She could see worry written all over Tarsea's face. "Relax! Leenea, Norri, and Tarah drilled me last night. I've got my cover story down pat. That story is actually easier for me to tell, than what really happened. The less I know and have to say about that portal, the happier I am." Kissing him on the cheek, she proceeded to the front door. She needed to really believe in what she told Tarsea. Alex knew she presented a brave facade.

Her two guards were waiting for her as she left the house, ready to escort her to the capital. She was just three steps into that journey when Tarsea communicated, *"You will do a great job. They will be too busy looking at your hot body."*

Hot body or not, she knew this interview was critical for her safety. Not only did her life depend on it, but her friends back on Ginkgo Terra as well. She took a deep breath and started walking to the Aster Province Palace with her assigned guards.

Chapter 16

Alex was mesmerized as she walked through the streets of the Aster Province. She had been carried unconscious through the streets when she arrived. The city streets were lined with all shades of purple plants and trees. No wonder the sky was violet, with all the purple foliage pollinating. There were plants she recognized and others that were new to her. In a world full of telepathic people, she wondered if there were books on plants she could look through.

The buildings were made of stone, but the artistry of their construction was amazing. Another contradiction of this new world she found herself in. They must have been built prior to the world fracturing again. It could have been a time when working with your hands was a valued skill. She could not imagine stone masonry being something these people aspired to. She wondered if Tarsea appreciated the beauty of his city or would merely walk through listening and responding to the different channels of communication that flowed into his head.

She looked up and saw The Palace in front of her, stopping in her tracks. Her guards stopped as well, keeping pace with their query. "It is really quite beautiful." She was referring to the four story magnificent building before her. She was careful to elongate her speech as Darden recommended.

"People come from around the Troyk world to witness the Aster Province Palace's beauty," the taller of her guards proudly stated. He stood a little straighter as he said it, bringing a smile to Alex's face. The Palace was a mauve color like the rest of the buildings, but it had marble inlays placed into its pillars. It sparkled as the sun's rays reflected off the shiny stone. The Palace seemed to shimmer.

Her two escorts skirted the crowd and she entered through doors that were obviously not for the general public. They were greeted as they entered by two men guarding the entrance. These men waved them on without any screening. Alex felt that was odd, after the failed assassination plot yesterday.

"Are you good to climb four flights of stairs?" the guard asked Alex as they reached the stairs. He was the talkative one, she did not recall the other escort saying a word to her.

"Yes," Alex responded, "that will be fine."

If the outside of the palace was magnificent, she was not sure how to describe the inside. The artwork was amazing, a kind of abstract art she had never seen. It seemed a perfect color complement to the stairs and fixtures in the grand hall. She continued to gaze at the work as she walked up more marble stairs. Alex would have to come back under better circumstances, so she could spend more time appreciating the treasures contained in this place.

She should be nervous, but the palace was truly overwhelming her senses. The communal channels she picked up were still speculating about yesterday's activities, business being conducted, and miscellaneous other conversations. No one seemed to notice her. It appeared that if she did not have face to face contact with someone, she faded in the background here as well.

They reached the top of the staircase and came upon a guard station. The talkative guard walked through first, followed by Alex and then the other guard. Once through security, they turned right, down a hallway full of opulence the likes she had never seen. She followed her guards and entered a room not far down that hallway. As they entered, an older gentleman and a striking woman stood.

The older man walked toward her, his hand extended. He was a good looking man, powerfully built, a full head of gray hair. The man looked damn good for his age. She reached out and he took her hand. "Welcome to my home, I am Jeryl Jarlyn."

Alex hoped she concealed her surprise that this attractive man was the mind controlling ruler of this province. She guessed she was expecting Ming the Magnificent from the 'Flash Gordon' movie.

She saw a momentary sadness spread across the man's face, quickly replaced with the welcoming grin she had noted earlier.

Alex addressed the Prime Ruler as he released her hand. "I am honored that you would take the time to meet me. Being new in town, I was surprised to have a personal audience with you. The Palace is everything people claim and so much more." Alex continued to be overwhelmed by the beauty she saw before her. Her thoughts shifted to Shirl and how much she would love to check out this place.

"Alexia," Jeryl Jarlyn smiled and turned to his left. "May I introduce you to Solfa Theffar? She runs our intelligence division. I like to have one of my staff attend my interviews with the young ladies that are brought before me. We are always looking for women to join our government."

Alex took a step toward the woman. She had rich chestnut hair, was a good six inches taller than her and had piercing blue eyes. "Solfa, it is nice to meet you as well."

She was surprised to see the woman who just linked with Tarsea through the newly identified warrior link at her interview with the Prime Ruler. She concentrated on not changing the expression on her face or giving her thoughts away. There was no such thing as coincidence.

"Welcome to the Aster Province," was all Solfa said. Tarsea had mentioned that she had told him not to worry about today's meeting. She was growing more and more nervous as her focus was on only one of these two individuals. Alex needed to remember that Solfa had linked into the warrior channel and that meant she was trustworthy.

Jarlyn led Alex to the chair next to where he had been sitting with Solfa. He motioned to the tea set and she shook her head.

"I meet all my young female subjects as they come of age. It is my way of welcoming them into Troyk society. We certainly did not want a lot of time to pass without meeting you. I hope you have recovered from any injuries you obtained from your fall. We will continue to speak out loud. We naturally do not want to tax your brain as it continues to heal."

Tarsea had mentioned last night that he did indeed meet with all the young women of the province, looking for his soul mate. That would explain the momentary change in Jarlyn's expression, when he knew she was not his soul mate.

"I am fine," Alex responded, "thank you. My aunt is considering relocating to the Aster Province. I wanted to see what it was like before I agreed to move with her. I love hiking and the mountain trails looked so inviting. It was embarrassing to be so clumsy and falling where I did. Thank goodness that Darden and Tarsea were there."

Alex could feel the pull on her brain. It was the result of Jarlyn trying to scan it with his mind control powers. She was glad Tarsea had described the sensation to her. Tarah's attempt to use mind control on her did not have this intensity.

"We are all thankful you have recovered so quickly. It was very generous of Zane Childers opening his home to you." Jeryl Jarlyn continued to scan her as he talked to her verbally.

"Yes, Zane and Leenea have been very welcoming. The experience has left a very favorable impression of your city. My aunt has joined me in the Childers household and we have decided to relocate here together."

The mind control pull on her brain had not weakened. Alex could also feel the static of the communal pathways increase. She knew she was losing her control over all the channels.

"Oh, no!" Alex cried as her nose started bleeding. "I am so sorry." She brought her palm up to her nose trying to stop the blood from ruining the rug or the furniture.

Solfa grabbed tissues and handed them to Alex. "I guess you are not as recovered as we had all wished."

"Thank you," Alex responded as she took the tissues. The pull on her brain had stopped. With the mind control pressure gone, Alex was able to grab control of the communal pathways once again.

"It has been a pleasure meeting you, Alexia. You will make a very nice addition to our community. You should go back to The Childers and rest. I am so sorry if we forced you out before you were truly healed." Obviously Jeryl Jarlyn was ending their audience. The interview had gone well. Fortunately, the nose bleed actually helped to reinforce the story she told.

"May I walk you out, Alexia?" Solfa Theffar asked her as the interview drew to a close.

"Please," Alex rose from her chair and walked with the woman as they left the room. They entered the hallway and Solfa gestured toward the stairs. Raine Narmouth was at the bottom. How very strange and disturbing.

"Alexia," Raine said, "what a wonderful surprise! I have a meeting with my commanding officer and looked up and there you were."

"Raine," Alexia said, "it is nice to see you again. This is Solfa Theffar. Solfa, this is Raine Narmouth. We both had accidents on the mountain trail the same day."

"Yes," Solfa responded, "we have met. You should not keep your commanding officer waiting, soldier."

Raine looked temporarily out of sorts, but recovered quickly. He did a funny little bow and continued on his way.

Solfa turned to Alex. "Would you mind if I accompany you back to the Childers' residence? After that nose bleed, I want to make sure you get back in one piece. Besides, I have a proposal to present to Tarsea."

Alex noticed that Solfa kept her eye on Raine, making sure he was on his way to his meeting as he said. It was odd that Solfa would track him as she did. Since she had a date with the man tomorrow and Solfa was the head of intelligence, maybe it was prudent to ask her about Raine.

"Solfa?" Alex asked. "Should I be concerned about Raine's attentions?"

"Honestly," Solfa responded, "I am not sure. He has never done anything off handed or illegal. I just for some reason have never trusted him. Humor me, let me walk you home."

"I would enjoy the company," Alex said as they left The Palace and started to Tarsea's parents' house. She still decided to guard what they talked about as they made their way through the city. Solfa informed her about the city and different sites as they walked. There was nothing about their discussion that raised any red flags as far as Alex was concerned.

"Tarsea, I am close to the house and I have Solfa Theffar with me. She asked to walk me back and has some type of proposal to discuss with you. Everything seemed to go well this morning with Jeryl Jarlyn." Alex leveraged the soul mate pathway to give Tarsea warning about Solfa joining her. She purposely did not mention the bloody nose or the presence of Raine Narmouth. Her mind was on what Solfa Theffar wanted of Tarsea.

Chapter 17

～

Tarsea opened the door as Alexandra and Solfa Theffar approached. He wrapped his arm around his soul mate, nuzzling her neck. *"I am never going to let you out of my sight again! I was so worried."*

"It's so good to be home. I didn't know what to do when Solfa asked to accompany me home." Alex responded using the soul mate channel.

Those words brought Tarsea back to the latest possible crises at hand, the presence of Solfa Theffar. He had no idea what the head of intelligence for Jeryl Jarlyn wanted to talk with him about. The fact that they connected through what could possibly be the warrior link troubled him.

"Welcome to our home, Solfa," Tarsea graciously said, "please come in." He extended his arm, motioning for her to follow him and Alexandra.

He walked her and his little pixie to his father's study. The small confines of the room would make it appear he was in control of the discussion. This woman held a tremendous amount of power in the city. Tarsea wanted to create the impression he had dominance here, as they entered into any discussion she wanted to initiate.

"Where is everyone?" Alexandra inquired.

"Darden, Koel, and Starc were in strategic locations around The Palace to catch you exiting. They held back when they saw you were with Solfa. You were followed home at a discrete distance. Mom and Dad took Norri sightseeing. Tolfer is in the kitchen preparing lunch. I wanted him nearby to see if he could hear Solfa through the closed link or if I am the only one who can hear her. The link started similarly with Tolfer."

"Please, have a seat," Tarsea addressed Solfa as he pointed to one of the chairs that stood before his father's desk. He had Alexandra sit in the second chair. Tarsea sat behind the desk, the symbolic place of power. He folded his hands and placed them on the table. "What can I do for you?"

Alexandra looked at Tarsea and then at Solfa, looking very uncomfortable. "Should I be here?" Alexandra asked Solfa. He was not pleased she had asked the woman, not him through their channel.

Solfa looked at Alexandra with an odd expression. "It is up to Tarsea whether he wishes you here."

"She stays," Tarsea answered. "Now, what is this about?" Tarsea knew he was bordering on being rude. He had not expected to have to deal with Solfa. His plans were to make love with Alexandra when she got home from her interview.

Before Solfa responded, there was the second major disturbance in the communal channels in the past two days. News that Prime Hosp had died was being communicated, both through official channels and informal chatter.

"Well, things just got more complicated," Solfa commented, referring to the news through the communal links.

Tarsea looked at Alexandra to see how she was handling the telepathic traffic across the various channels. She was rubbing her temple, but appeared to be managing the flow of communication. It would be best to get more herbs into his soul mate to help her manage the volume of activity in the pathways.

Before he used the familial channel to contact his brother, Tolfer came in with several mugs of tea. He handed Alexandra the herbal mix, while everyone else was served a basic herbal tea. Rather than leaving, his brother propped himself on the end of their father's desk. Alexandra started to sip the herbal beverage and Tarsea could already see the tension in her body reduce. Her shoulders were more relaxed, rather than almost touching her ears.

"Solfa, why did you want to meet with me?" Tarsea still had not received an answer to his previous question.

"Yesterday evening we communicated via a channel I had never experienced before. Your parting words to me piqued my interest. It also influenced what I reported to Jeryl and my recommendation to him." Solfa took another sip of tea, as if she had not dropped a loaded devise into Tarsea's lap. He tried to keep a stoic expression in response to what she said.

"What exactly did you report back to Jarlyn?" Tarsea inquired, while at the same time communicated to his soul mate not to panic.

Solfa looked at him with her piercing eyes. He did not doubt she could get anyone to confess to a crime. "There is no evidence whatsoever that you had anything to do with the assassination plot. I voiced my opinion that you were a valuable resource that could be better leveraged by the government. I also mentioned I was concerned that Prime Adholm was going to paint a very different picture. His judgment was possibly clouded because you had messed around with his daughter and then dumped her."

"Did Prime Adholm report as you suspected?" Tarsea was almost afraid to hear the answer. He had never trusted Prime Adholm.

Solfa laughed. "No, he reported that you had too much invested in the current government to do anything as stupid as supporting Prime Hosp. He did use colorful language about your morals and not being able to keep a certain part of your anatomy under control." The woman once again glanced at Alex. Tarsea did not like how she was looking at his soul mate.

"Solfa," Alex joined the conversation, "you mentioned that you had an offer to present to Tarsea. What is the opportunity?" It appeared she was as frustrated as he was, wanting to know what the woman wanted.

Solfa gave his little minx yet another odd look and then turned back to Tarsea. "You and your family wield a lot of power in this government and in the business community. I also know that you have been using this influence to help certain targeted individuals leave the Troyk universe."

Tarsea immediately replied, "I do not have a clue what you are talking about." This discussion was taking a dangerous turn. He glanced at his brother, who was still as a statue.

Solfa shook her head and grinned. "Your network is not as good as you think it is. Do you actually believe you were able to save all those people without some intervention outside your group?"

All Tarsea could do was stare at her. He was not sure how to respond. His blood pressure increased and he could almost hear it rushing through his body.

He did not have to wait long for Solfa to continue. "Two weeks ago your group was able to rescue someone who had been printing pamphlets calling for the end of mind control. Fortunately, one of my men had been observing the man until we had undisputed evidence against him. Let us say for the sake of argument, that this intelligence officer has reservations against the practice of mind control. He looked the other way when Starc and Darden collected the man to send him through the portal to another world."

Tarsea swore under his breath. "What is your proposal?"

"There are many factions that want change. Some work within the system, others work outside it. Peaceful change is easier if it comes from the inside. I want you to join the intelligence community. Jarlyn believes you are loyal and you will be able to continue to appear that way. However, now you have more internal resources you can leverage." Solfa was giving him an opportunity that was too good to be true. The question still remained whether she could be trusted.

"How many voices did you hear in the link you connected through last night?" Tarsea asked her through the closed channel.

"As I walked here with Alexia, I believe I heard Darden, Starc, and Koel. Earlier this morning, I also heard that intelligence officer, I had mentioned earlier linking in. Naturally, I did not share with him anything about the channel. I wanted to talk to you first."

"Holy shit!" exclaimed Tolfer. Obviously his brother heard Solfa through the link. He was impressed how composed his brother had been throughout the discussion to this point.

"What?" Alexandra demanded. "What is going on?"

"I just told Tarsea through whatever channel we communicated through last night, that I heard Darden, Starc, and Koel talking through that link as we were walking here. In addition, one of my young officers also linked in." Solfa looked at Tolfer, "I assume you can access the link as well from your reaction."

As Solfa was explaining orally to Alexandra, Tarsea was also communicating through the soul mate link. *"I am sorry, baby. I can transmit to you what I say through the link, but what comes back I will have to transmit after I receive it. There will always be a delay to bring you into the conversation."*

Solfa again looked at Alexandra with an intense stare. He really wished he understood why she continued to look at his soul mate in such a manner. Having his father's large desk between them no longer seemed like a great idea.

"You need to understand my motivation," Solfa informed them. "My mother had a cousin who spoke out against mind control many years ago. She left this world when it got too dangerous. My mother was deeply affected by the loss of her cousin. I was raised with a hatred of the practice. Early on I knew I had to be cautious related to what I did about that hatred. That is why I got involved in the government. It was my way of trying to change things where I saw opportunities. I also had to make some tough decisions over the years regarding who would live and who would die in order to maintain my cover. It has not been easy."

"You don't think she's talking about one of the people who went through the portal with my parents, do you?" Alexandra asked him through the soul mate channel.

Before he had a chance to respond, Alexandra asked Solfa the question that must have been plaguing her. "What was your mother's cousin's name?"

⌒⊙

Solfa gave Alexandra a poignant glance before she responded. "Starta, Starta Montiff Gerrit. I believe she was the sister of the woman you claim to be your aunt. When Starta went through the portal I was about ten years old."

"Alexandra, you need to control your emotions. I will get Norri back here as fast as possible." Alex took a deep breath and did as Tarsea suggested. Her aunt would be here soon and she did have her soul mate here in the meantime.

"Solfa," Alex asked, "is your mother still alive? Norri said she has some distant relatives somewhere in the province." She was quite proud of herself, she was able to ask the question calmly.

"Yes. I have put off mentioning to her that Norri is in town. They had lost touch after Starta left. I believe it was just too painful to keep the relationship going. Norri and Starta were twins, but there was a special relationship between my mom and Starta."

Alex took a sip of the herbal beverage and then concentrated on Solfa. Her desire to tell this woman who she really was, was too much to bear. Solfa had linked into the warrior channel, so she had to be trustworthy. She must have given away her intent because her soul mate almost immediately gave her a warning through their closed link. *"Hold off on trying to link with her, Alexandra. We still do not know if we can trust her."*

She disregarded Tarsea's warning. "My *mother's name was Starta*." Not knowing if the familial link would work between second cousins, or whatever their relationship was. If Solfa was lying about their relationship, she would not be able to receive the communication anyway. What did she have to lose?

Solfa's eyes grew larger and started to water with tears that were about to fall. Both women got up and hugged. This was the second family member she had found in the last three days. She imagined she'd soon meet a third, when she met Solfa's mother.

"I knew you had to be her daughter. As soon as I saw you, it took me back to when I was a little girl. You look so much like your mother." Solfa talked to Alex through the familial link. Hearing another member of her family connecting with her in such a manner warmed Alex's heart.

As she held her cousin, Alex finally realized what her life's calling was. "I want to be an intelligence officer and help in the cause that resulted in my parents having to leave this universe."

"Absolutely not!" Tarsea growled.

"You are not the boss of me! I am going into the family business." She knew she sounded like a child. Alex wanted this more than she ever wanted anything. It was important to make a mark on the world and this would be her way of doing it. She had finally found her life's work.

"Alexandra, I thought we were going to make decisions together. You are too new to this world, you need a period of adjustment." There was a desperation in Tarsea's voice through their link. She needed to let her soul mate know how important this was to her.

"Tarsea, I am your soul mate, but I am not an invalid. The sooner I get involved and immersed in this world, the faster I will adjust." She hoped she sounded more mature this time around and Tarsea would listen. Alex was also careful not to give away she was from another world.

"Wait a minute!" Solfa broke into the argument between her and Tarsea. "Did you say you are soul mates?"

"Alex, you have to be more careful who you blurt out we are soul mates to!" Tarsea chastised her. As he was raking her over the coals, he was also addressing Solfa. "Solfa, we are newly found soul mates."

Solfa looked between her and Tarsea. Alex knew she was debating whether to ask the big question or not. "You know I have to ask," Solfa confessed. "Has your relationship hit a certain point where you have gone through the evolutionary change?"

Alex could tell how uncomfortable her cousin was with the question. For the first time since she met her, her cheeks were tinged with a red blush. She was also impressed at how discretely Solfa was able to phrase her inquiry. There was a lot she could learn from this woman, her cousin.

"Yes," Alex responded, "we have taken the next evolutionary developmental leap. Solfa, I should be able to read people's thoughts, as well as protect myself from mind control."

"So, you were able to negate Jarlyn's mind control pull this morning?" Solfa asked.

"I could feel the pull," Alex answered, "but could naturally block anything he wanted to pick-up. Because of the evolutionary change, I will be that much more of an asset to your organization.

"I should also be able to communicate with a closed link with anyone or read their thoughts eventually. Although I cannot link into the closed channel you now are part of, I can talk to you through the familial channel or to Tarsea via the soul mate channel. I can go into places, and generally not be noticed. I would rock as an intelligence officer." She knew she sounded more and more desperate. Hopefully that desperation would be viewed as passion and Solfa would take her on.

Her cousin looked at Alex critically. God, she loved that fact that she had a cousin. Solfa was giving her the same piercing look she gave her this morning during the interview. She could almost see the gears in her cousin's head go around.

"Alexandra, it takes years of training and you do not know the ins and outs of Troyk culture yet." Tarsea was still trying to talk her out of what she knew was going to add purpose to her life.

Alex walked over to Tarsea, sat on his lap and kissed him. *"I am doing this, Tarsea. I have a strong soul mate and I want to be as strong as he is. It is important to me to make a difference, to change the world that drove my folks ultimately to their deaths."*

Tarsea kissed her and said, "I still do not like the idea of you being put in danger. Maybe after you are more familiar with our customs, as well as better managing all the telepathic channels. Solfa, you have to admit, your people have years of training."

"Tarsea," Solfa responded, "I monitored all the communal channels when I walked out of The Palace with Alexia. There was absolutely no chatter about her or to her. The same was true as we walked here. That is what I look for when considering someone to be part of our intelligence community."

"For once in my life, being invisible is a huge plus! I can go into a bar, gather information and no one will even know I am there." Alex decided she would share what she could contribute to Solfa's organization. The part of her, she once wanted to change in her old life, was going to be a benefit in her intelligence work.

Her cousin's expression softened. "Not quite, Alexia. However, you do not make an impression, which is a positive. You are a true chameleon, you blend into the background. Can she really read people's thoughts?" Alex did not take offense that her cousin addressed that last question to Tarsea.

Tarsea nodded his head. "With time and training, yes. It is yet another pathway that soul mates possess. I was actually able to hear you call me a 'man whore' in your thoughts last night."

Tolfer started laughing and Solfa face turned redder than it had before. Alex was still smarting about his relationship with Chartail. The fact that everyone in the province knew about his sexual escapades did not thrill her. When she looked at Tarsea, she could tell he wished he could have taken that comment back.

"Alexia," Solfa said, "thank goodness you are soul mates. I was going to warn you off Tarsea because of his track record with women. All morning I was trying to ascertain if you were my cousin. Once you confirmed you were, I was not happy that you appeared to have a relationship with this man. Now that I know the true nature of your bonding, I feel much better. I guess the next thing we need to figure out is how to leverage you and Tarsea into my organization."

"When do I start?" Alex asked. She felt Tarsea's grip on her tighten.

Their conversation got interrupted as Tarsea's parents and her aunt Norri returned home.

"I think we need to move this into the common room. Everyone is probably hungry anyway." Tarsea stood, taking her with him. He took her hand as they left the study.

"We will continue this discussion in bed later tonight."

Alex smiled *"No, we won't. We'll be too busy doing other things. It's all decided anyway."* She reached up and gave him a kiss on the cheek.

Solfa used their familial pathway. *"We will talk about how we can use you in our intelligence community later."*

Alex's mood soared as they made their way to the common room. Solfa was going to bring her on as an intelligence operative.

She had a real family, a soul mate, a new world to conquer, and a true calling to dedicate this part of her life to. Now she just had to figure out how to turn herself into James Bond.

⌒○

Who in the world was James Bond and what did he mean to Alexandra? He caught a fragment of a thought from his soul mate as they made their way to the common room to greet his parents and her aunt. Tonight when they were alone in bed, he was going to find out. He also needed to dissuade her from endangering herself by going into intelligence work.

Things were moving too fast, Tarsea felt he was losing control. There were two more people who could communicate through the closed link. He was no longer sure how secure this channel was with Solfa and this unknown intelligence officer having access. Regardless of what Darden said, he was still concerned.

Alexandra broke away from him and hugged her aunt. The woman looked as relieved as Tarsea was to have her back from the interview unscathed. For the first time, Tarsea wondered what would happen to Norri if she lost such a close relative again. He had come to care for the woman in the very short time he had known her. It was probably a result of his soul mate's feelings for her aunt.

He certainly did not like this latest development where Alexandra wanted to become an intelligence operative. Regardless, he was still considering Solfa's offer.

"Norri, do you remember a young cousin here in the Aster Province about the time my mother went through the portal?" Alexandra was driving to get Solfa into the fold before Tarsea was comfortable with another addition. She boldly moved forward before he could hold her back using their private channel to communicate his concerns.

Norri glanced behind Tarsea, where Solfa was lagging behind him. She had a questioning expression on her face as she moved to approach the woman. It almost appeared that this forceful intelligence officer was afraid of not being recognized by her own family.

"Solfalynn?" Alexandra's aunt cried out the question. Norri embraced the woman before she even responded. Tarsea heard his soul mate's cry as the two women came together.

"It is just plain Solfa now. I never thought I would see you again. We feared you entered the portal after your sister. You just disappeared, Norri!"

"I could no longer stay here after Starta left. There was so much chatter in the communal pathways about Benko and his followers. Every time Jarlyn addressed us, I thought I would go mad. I needed to get away and make a clean break of things. Is your mother still living?" Norri took her palm and wiped away the tears from her face.

"Tarsea, I finally have a family." His soul mate joined the two women, tears still falling from her eyes. Alexandra was not the only one discovering her lost family. Norri seemed as impacted emotionally as his soul mate was.

It was at this point he made the decision he had to believe that people who joined the closed link had to be trustworthy. If Solfa proved to be a traitor, he was not sure Alexandra would be able to handle it. He had to have faith that the legends associated with the warrior channel were true, if indeed they were dealing with the legendary link. No one was more honorable and reliable than the individuals that guarded the true leader of the Troyk Universe, according to the stories he grew up hearing.

"Darden, Starc, Koel, please come to my parents' home. We need to discuss our next steps. I also have someone to introduce you to." Tarsea needed to get everyone back on track after the uncertainty of the last several days and the new information that came forward with Alexandra's unexpected entry into the Troyk Universe. It was also time to finally talk about Benko Jarlyn.

Norri sat next to Solfa, with Alexandra on the other side of her newly found cousin. As always, his mother was handing out beverages. She made sure that his soul mate had the herbs she needed to help manage the pathways. Tarsea's heart was warmed when he saw his mother brush away some of the leftover tears on his little pixie's cheek and kiss her.

His thoughts were interrupted by Solfa's question. "Should I have Karlon join us? He is the intelligence officer, I told you that had linked with me via the closed channel."

Tarsea considered her question for a moment and then responded. "Invite him via the closed link and we will see what happens. The others should be here any minute."

❧

"While we are waiting," Alex said, "how did the house hunting go?" Her aunt seemed a little off, she could not figure out why.

"There was this adorable cottage that Tolfer and I first saw that would have been perfect. I ended up signing a lease for a garden home further down the street."

Alex frowned, "Norri, why didn't you get the cottage?"

"Alex," Tolfer answered, "a mind control telepath was at the cottage and told her she would be happier at the other residence."

Solfa took Alex's hand. "That is how mind control telepathic power works, it is very subtle. You think you want one thing, but when they are done with you, you want something else."

"That's terrible! Are the results permanent?" After what happened yesterday with Jeryl Jarlyn, she was concerned about her aunt.

"Yes, but for that decision only," Tarsea answered. "It is just like when you change your mind naturally. Unless there is new information or some kind of stimulus to restart your decision making process, it is like any other decision you make. There is no lasting damage to the brain. They only impact you when you are making a decision."

"How did they come to power? Why didn't more people fight against it?" Alex had heard of mind control telepathic influences, but now that it impacted her aunt, it became very real.

"Benko and his followers tried," Solfa answered. "Mind control telepathic abilities exist in a small percentage of the population, but grew to power by their ability to manipulate. Benko tried to reason with his father about mind control and other governmental practices. Jarlyn and others like him feel they are superior because of their abilities. Their belief is the Supreme Being gave them this additional talent to oversee those of weaker telepathic capacity. In the end, he escaped with your mother and other followers with their lives."

"What other practices were Benko and my parents fighting, Solfa?"

"Alexia, how about we fight one battle at a time," Solfa answered wearily. It would appear that her cousin was beginning to show the stress of the day.

Alex could see her cousin give Tarsea a look. She knew she was being given bits and pieces about what was wrong with the Troyk Universe. Honestly, she was a little relieved. Alex had enough to deal with at the present time. Any more would be too much for her brain to handle until she could manage all the telepathic channels.

"All right, I can live with that for now. But I do have to function in this world, as if I cannot resist mind control." She turned to Leenea and Zane. "How have you managed all these years? You must have had mind control telepathic individuals telling you what to do."

Zane ran his hands down his face before he answered Alex's question. "Many times we did exactly what the mind control telepath wanted. If it was something we felt strongly about we purposely brought about that stimulus that Tarsea had mentioned. When we did something contrary to what we were told, it was clear something external allowed us to change our mind."

Leenea laughed, "You would be surprised how often I left my wallet at home."

Alex was satisfied for now, she knew she would be able to live in this world with the guidance of those around her. She could not imagine living here, not knowing if decisions she made were hers or those of a mind control telepath.

The aroma coming out of the kitchen was starting to overwhelm her senses. "How does lunch sound? I am starving again."

Tarsea smiled at his little pixie. For such a small creature, she could certainly pile away the food. He was actually hungry and ready to eat as well. He got up and patted his brother on the back.

"I will pull lunch out of the oven and we can all eat as we talk," Tolfer announced as he left the common room for the kitchen. Tarsea was still amazed that Tolfer had been able to link into the closed channel. He was always so concerned about the comfort of others. Tolfer never got involved in any of the covert missions Tarsea was involved in. The others arrived as Tarsea finished his thought.

Darden entered the common room, while Koel and Starc went to assist Tolfer. It was not long before everyone had a plate of food on their laps. They were ready to start discussing the current status and the next steps they were going to take. He noted Alexandra was digging into her lunch. Good, she was going to need all the energy she could get for what he had planned for this evening. With those thoughts pushed to the back of his mind, he needed to get the discussion started.

"Prime Hosp is dead and according to Solfa," Tarsea said, "there are no clues regarding who was part of the assassination plot." He thought it best to start with the most urgent item first, since it was still going to plague them until the guilty parties were identified.

Solfa nodded, agreeing with his assessment. "I have helped interview over two dozen individuals. We had at least one mind control telepath with us at all times. Through all the interviews, we know no more than when we started." There was a knock on the door. "That must be Karlon." Solfa took a sip of her tea, waiting for her associate to enter before she continued.

His father answered the door. When he returned, he was followed by a nondescript young man. Solfa was not exaggerating when she had mentioned the benefits of having agents who could blend in and not be recognizable later. Tarsea looked at his soul mate through new eyes.

"This is intelligence officer Karlon Flonder. He has supported my efforts to assist covert rescues to the best of our abilities." Solfa turned to Darden and Starc with a gleam in her eyes. "He witnessed your mission from two weeks ago, when you escorted Stellas Harstrong through the portal."

Tarsea chuckled when he saw the stunned expressions on both men's faces. "It appears we had assistance we did not know about. Both Solfa and Karlon have linked into our closed channel. They are now part of the team. We also have access directly into Troyk Intelligence."

Fortunately, there were no challenges to what Tarsea just communicated. There was no question they had fallen into a windfall.

"What are the next steps in tracking down the people who were involved in the attempt on Jarlyn's life?" His father knew they were not out of the woods yet and as usual wanted as much information as possible.

Solfa took a deep breath and looked at his soul mate. "Formal interviews are not getting us anywhere. It is time we hit the streets and listen to what is not being communicated through communal channels. I need as many of my intelligence people out in public listening to conversations that are not meant to be overheard."

"I want to help." That was all Alexandra said. The look on her face broke Tarsea's heart. He had no idea how he was going to talk her into backing down from her plans.

"Alexandra and I are soul mates. The stories are true that soul mates are able to listen in on the thoughts of others. Unlike mind control telepathic abilities, we cannot influence what someone does with their thoughts." Tarsea thought it was important to draw that distinction between what they could do versus the practice they were all fighting against.

"We need to start referring to Alexandra as either Alexia or Alex, even in private. It will be too easy to slip up and call her the wrong name in public or through the communal pathways." Solfa was right, Tarsea nodded in agreement.

Solfa gave him a look whether she could continue. It was reassuring that she respected he was in charge of this group. There may be power struggles down the road, but for now it seemed she was willing to take a follower role.

She continued after receiving Tarsea's approval to continue with her debrief. "I would like Alexia and Tarsea to start being seen in public together. They can listen to what people are thinking, as well as Alexia can over hear verbal conversations." Solfa took her cousin's hand. "Are you ready for this, Alexia?"

His soul mate got a big smile on her face. "I was born ready!" She came over to Tarsea and sat on his lap. "Can we start tonight?" There was no question in his mind that she was going to leverage everything in her soul mate arsenal to get her way. He would make sure he was there when she went out on her missions, if he could not stop them ahead of time. He would also reap the benefits at night in their bed as she continued to convince him she needed to be an intelligence officer.

"Darden," Tarsea addressed his best friend, "I believe you have some information to shed about our closed link that as of now has two new members linking in."

"It is not a closed communal pathway," Darden informed the group, "it is the warrior link."

"That is impossible," Norri commented, "you have to be mistaken. I know I said your closed pathway was odd the other day, but you are leaping into make believe."

Darden shook his head, "Norri, it is the warrior pathway, there is no mistake. I originally thought it was the start of a new communal pathway as well, but it did not expand as public pathways do. It takes priority over both familial pathways and communal channels. The last time I was on Ginkgo Terra, I used it to link with Benko Jarlyn. The reception was as clear as oral communication, I had never experienced anything like it."

"Benko Jarlyn," Solfa cried, "you are in contact with him? Our nightmare may soon be over?" He was not surprised by her reaction. Benko's name was a rally call in all underground movements for over two decades. Most groups were fueled with just the thought the man was alive and would one day return.

"Let us not get ahead of ourselves yet," Tarsea reasoned. "We still have a lot of ground work to do before it is safe for Benko to come home. Our first priority has to be catching who masterminded the failed assassination of his father. Until we do that and security is relaxed, there is no way to advance our cause."

He could tell Solfa was considering his words. She finally nodded her consent. "Can you and Alexia start tonight by going out in public? See what you can hear. Jarlyn is limiting portal access and is having every single incoming event horizon investigated. Even when there is a planned return of a crystal telepath."

That information reinforced the criticality of finding who planned an attempt on Jarlyn's life. There would be no rescue missions or bringing back any of Alex's friends until that person was in custody and dealt with.

"All time off has been canceled for the CT Guards," Starc shared with the group. "I made two trips to the portal today before meeting up with everyone to cover Alex's return from The Palace."

He could feel Alexandra getting restless. "Take me out to dinner tonight, Tarsea. I want to see more of the city. We need to find out who was behind the assassination attempt, so the security around the portal will be relaxed."

Tarsea reluctantly agreed. He would have given anything to keep Alexandra shut in a little longer. However, she did need to start assimilating into her new world. The more he gave in to her where he had control, the easier it would be to manage her activity as an intelligence officer. He imagined Solfa would be willing to negotiate greater involvement of Tarsea and a much lesser involvement where his soul mate was concerned.

"We will go out for the first sitting of dinner," Tarsea finally responded to Alexandra's request and Solfa's order. He could see Alex's confusion regarding his comment. "The first seating of dinner is casual, like how you would dress for lunch. Women dress up for the second seating. It is a time to be seen and stand out. Your clothing currently is appropriate for the first seating of dinner."

"First seating it is then," Alexandra said, as she almost bounced on his lap with excitement.

Tonight would be their first date and her first intelligence assignment. He had every intention of overwhelming her senses with all things sensual, giving her no time or desire to be a spy.

Chapter 18

~

Alex held Tarsea's hand as they made their way to the meeting place, nearest to his parents' house. He made sure she wore the most nondescript outfit his mother had purchased for her. In addition, the tunic hung, rather than hugging her curves. She actually felt more comfortable in these nondescript outfits. When she wore the form fitting outfits, she did not like the way men looked at her. For the first time in her life, she could understand how Shirl felt. The evening attire that had been described to her, would make what she is wearing now seem like a potato sack.

She loved walking through the streets of Aster Province. Phoenix was lovely in the spring, but the rest of the year it was brown and hot. These streets abound with color. True, it was shades of purple, but it was still beautiful. There were various types of lavender, lilacs, asters, orchids, iris and petunias.

"It is beautiful here. I was wondering why there were no cars. Everyone walks and that's great, but I thought you brought back technology from other worlds." Alexandra voiced the question that was plaguing her mind since she walked to and from The Palace. She actually liked the quiet associated with having no cars driving along the streets.

Tarsea seemed to be considering Alex's question. He always took great care in what he told her about this new world. *"We take what scientific advancements we feel would enhance the Troyk universe. For distances we leverage clean energy burning trams. We do not burn fossil fuels here. I would not be surprised if one of the agents burning those fuels produced what attacks our telepathic brains."*

Alex pondered what Tarsea said and it made sense. She loved her car and could not imagine the people in her old world would give up their cars so easily.

Sure, they created pollution, but she had never considered that it killed her parents and would have ultimately killed her. She knew she could never go back to her former world. This made her even more determined to make the Troyk Universe a better and safer place.

They reached the meeting place and Tarsea bent over to kiss her cheek. "Do you want to take a walk on one of the trails before we grab a bite?"

Alex looked at the park with wonder. Wow, she was definitely not in Kansas anymore! The park was blooming with color, it was a purple wonderland. The sign in front of her showed there were six paths to choose from. She thought walking a little longer would reduce the stress she was feeling.

This was really her first venture into Troyk society. Although Tarsea was next to her, she could not control her nerves. Maybe she was just having first date jitters, which was ridiculous because they had already made love. The bottom line was she was nervous about managing the communal pathways in public, trying her new mind reading ability, and being around people in general.

Taking a quick look at the park, she saw a trail full of heather. "Let us take the 'Lover's Path.'" From the park directory, that was the path with the heather that caught her eye. She was also conscious that she said 'let us', rather than 'let's' when she spoke out loud. It still sounded weird to her ear.

"Great choice," Tarsea said, "and very appropriate." He took her hand and led her to the path she had chosen. There were a number of couples who walked along the trail.

"What are the odds that any of these couples are soul mates?" Alex asked Tarsea as she eyed other couples. She tried to see if there were little nuances in their behaviors that could have marked them as soul mates.

"Having lived whole my life with soul mates and not having known my parents were ones, I would not venture to guess. If there are any, they are keeping it a secret."

He tightened his grip on her hand. Alex continued to look at the couples as they passed. She was fascinated watching them, wondering what stories they had to share. How many of them were like Zane and Leenea, hiding their true relationship? Were their choices made for them by mind control telepathic people or were they able to circumvent the compulsions that were attacking their brains as soul mates could?

"*Tarsea,*" Alex said, "*that is so sad. It is something that should be celebrated, not hidden away in fear. We are going to change this world so soul mates will be able to come out of the closet.*"

"*Out of the what?*"

Obviously, that was not a phrase used in this world. Alex did not want to take the time to explain it to Tarsea. "*Never mind. Let's enjoy the beauty of this path and then grab dinner, I'm starving.*"

They started toward the beginning of the trail when she saw Raine Narmouth coming in their direction.

"Alexia," Raine called, "another coincidence running into you again."

"Another?" Tarsea asked. She did not like the look he was giving her at this point. To be honest with herself, she should have told him about her last contact with him. His reaction to her accepting a date with him was so explosive, she was a little apprehensive to add fuel to the fire.

"Yes," Alex responded to Tarsea, "I ran into him at The Palace after my appointment with our Prime Ruler." She could tell Tarsea was not happy she did not share this information with him sooner. "How was your meeting with your superior?"

"Thank you for asking," Raine said. "I found out I was promoted to Captain of the CT Guard."

"Congratulations!" Alex replied to Raine. "I am sure it is well deserved." She had no idea what a CT Guard was, she would have to ask Tarsea after he calmed down. That was assuming he was still talking to her.

"Narmouth," Tarsea sneered, "if you will excuse us, we are heading to dinner."

"Not a problem," Raine answered. "Alexia, I will pick you up tomorrow around 11 a.m. It should be a lovely day for the zoo."

Raine continued walking, leaving Alex with a very irritated Tarsea. He did not say a word, just grabbed her hand and quickened their pace toward the restaurant. He was no longer the attentive lover, but the scowling man who tried to control her actions.

She was relieved when they finally arrived at their destination. They were immediately seated and handed menus. The items were not too different from what she could get at home. Only the preparation seemed the major difference.

Before they left the house, they had talked about how they were going to manage conversations at dinner in the restaurant. Since it was their first date in public, they would speak aloud, as other couples did. If there was critical information that needed to be shared, only then would they leverage the soul mate channel.

"Tarsea," Alex said, "I am sorry I did not mention seeing Raine at The Palace this morning. It was a coincidence, he had a meeting with his superior." She did not feel it was necessary to mention that Solfa said she did not trust the guy.

"I want to know every time you see him, even if it is in a crowded location and you just catch a glimpse of him. Starc has a history with Narmouth and it is not good."

Alex felt like they had spent enough time talking about Raine Narmouth. She needed to re-direct the conversation. Food always seemed to work where Tarsea was concerned.

"What should I order?" Alex asked. She had looked through the whole menu and was not sure what she should have.

"Order the keen chicken. It is one of their specialties. I think we should also limit our wine consumption to one glass tonight." Tarsea bit into a piece of bread that had just been delivered by one of the waiters.

Alex smiled, it would not be too smart to get sloshed on her first night out. Plus, when people drank, emotions tended to be exaggerated. She figured they had enough drama already for the evening.

"Are you picking up any thoughts from a channel you have not experienced yet? It will just be one voice and you will have to be looking at the person. You do not have to look at their face, focus on their head." Tarsea leveraged the soul mate channel this time around.

Alex concentrated on the people who were walking by, without being too obvious about it. She was only picking up communal chatter. Tarsea had explained earlier, it could take her longer to be able to pick up other's thoughts, since she had just started leveraging the telepathic channels.

"Not yet," she did not want to sound defeated. Maybe after they ate, she would try it again. Her growling stomach may have been too much of a distraction.

The waiter came by and they both telepathically placed their orders. It was a very weird experience to order along with everyone else through the communal pathway. She could hear others ordering as she and the waiter conversed telepathically.

The wine came almost immediately, since the wine steward had her order as she was requesting it. She took a big swig from the glass, rather than a delicate sip. It was delicious, but did nothing to calm her nerves. She took a piece of bread from the basket and started nibbling on it. Wine on an empty stomach was also not such a bright idea. Because of her size, she had a very low alcohol tolerance.

Out of the corner of her eye, she saw a bright orange flash and turned in that direction. A lovely blonde came into view, wearing a bright shirt and a very short skirt in the same color. There was no way she could ever be an intelligence agent, that woman stood out like a sore thumb.

"Oh, shit!" Alex turned to Tarsea after he said those words. He took a bigger swig of his wine than she had earlier.

She was just about to ask him what the problem was when the woman she had noticed stopped right in front of their table.

"Well, well, look who we have here. If it is not the dick head himself." Alex looked at the woman and then back to Tarsea. She had an inkling who this woman was. This evening was just getting better and better.

"Chartail, how about not making a scene." Tarsea looked very uncomfortable and Alex could understand why. Her instincts were right, it was the woman he just dumped.

The woman in question now looked at Alex and gave her the once over. "You are certainly not his type. This relationship will not last long. I would not get too comfortable with him if I were you."

"What a bitch! You slept with this she-beast?" The woman was actually raising her nose to Alex and she did not like it. Shirl was more beautiful than this tramp and she would never treat another woman this way.

"Alex, be smart." That was all Tarsea had to say. She could already hear the communal pathways full of chatter about the confrontation. It was odd the conversations were focused on Chartail and Tarsea, as if she was not even there. She would have to tell Solfa about that later.

"Excuse me, I just got into town and am friends of Tarsea and his family. Who are you again?" Alex was actually proud of the self-control she showed.

She managed to hold herself back from saying what she really wanted to tell this witch.

"My name is Chartail and I was Tarsea's girlfriend until you had your spill on the mountain."

Alex could not help herself, she started to laugh. It was the most ridiculous statement she had ever heard. "Honey, there has to be an easier way to meet men than falling, losing consciousness, and being carried through the streets of the city."

Chartail had the grace to at least blush at what Alex had said. The gorgeous blonde looked at her in a different light. Her haughty expression changed to a friendlier one.

"I am sorry. You are new in town. It is not your fault you got duped by the asshole you are having dinner with." Chartail was now talking to Alex, rather than talking down to her.

"Chartail, I am not sure how to respond to that. Thanks?" Alex was really loving this conversation. She had never been the other woman before.

Tarsea's former girlfriend got a big smile on her face. It almost appeared to Alex she had come up with a brilliant idea. "Listen, I am having lunch with friends here the day after tomorrow. Why not join us. You can meet some more people and broaden your choices of folks you hang out with and the men you date." Alex did not miss the look she threw Tarsea when she made that last comment.

"Absolutely not, Alexandra," Tarsea growled through the soul mate channel.

She loved this side of him. The growling, snarling and other sounds he made when he was displeased. It brought out the primal side of him. She was sure they would spar tonight about her accepting yet another invitation he was not happy about.

"Wow, I would love to! I do not know anyone in the city other than Tarsea, his friends and family. It would be great to meet some other people." Alex smiled at Chartail. At the same time she communicated to Tarsea, *"We are talking about me getting close to Chartail for the same reason you were sleeping with her. Her father is one of the most important men in the city and very close to Jarlyn himself."*

"Great, should we say noon? I cannot wait to tell the girls who they are going to meet. For some reason I think we are going to be close friends." Chartail did a fake kiss on both sides of Alex's face and then sashayed off. She managed to give Tarsea a look that could kill before she left. Alex had really enjoyed the repartee that just occurred.

"Boy, wasn't your old girlfriend a breath of fresh air? What was that fake kissing all about? You lasted seven months with Miss Sunshine?"

"It is all part of the job," Tarsea said with a smirk on his face. Alex kicked him under the table, just as their entrees arrived.

Alex dug into her keen chicken, which was outstanding. For some reason, food tasted better in the Troyk Universe. The wine that Tarsea selected was a perfect complement to the dish. She felt much calmer. It was questionable whether it was the wine or the triumphant discussion with Chartail that made her feel better. The communal channels were not creating any unmanageable static in her brain. All in all, it had been a very successful venture out.

"What exactly do you do for a living, Tarsea?" It was general date talk and she was not really sure what he did for a living.

"My father runs a business, which I help him with. I am also assisting a number of the Prime Representatives."

"What does that entail?" She actually found this discussion very interesting and well over due.

"I research a number of items that are up for votes or being considered for legislation. Dad and I also leverage the position to get various obstacles that impede our business to be removed with legislation."

Not too different from things at home. The man is a fucking lobbyist, for goodness sake. Well, at least he had a side job of trying to bring down the government.

They finished off their meals and the check arrived. Tarsea got a funny look on his face.

"We have to go, pixie, there has been a development and I need to be home to coordinate efforts." He threw some cash on the check and got up.

"What happened?" Whatever it was, it had distracted him from the mood he had previously been in. He was calling her a pixie again.

"They think they have found Prime Hosp's wife and are about to arrest her. We are going to see if we can get to her before they do."

Tarsea walked over and pulled her chair back so she could get up.

"We should head home. I told my parents, we could only be gone for about two hours. We certainly do not want them to worry," Tarsea said to her for the benefit of those around them, in case their silent departure would draw attention. Alex knew she could learn a lot from this man about appearances and telepathic channels.

She walked beside him as they left the restaurant. They had planned a quiet night at home, but it appeared their plans had just been hijacked by the Hosp assassination attempt. What more could happen today?

Chapter 19

Tarsea knew he was in a foul mood when they got back to his parents' house. He had not expected Chartail to show up at dinner, for Alexandra to have plans for lunch with her, or for her to have a date with Raine Narmouth. On top of everything else, he also had to deal with the latest in the Hosp fiasco. All he wanted was to get his soul mate into bed and work off his frustrations. The latest closed link communication made that desire impossible for now.

Starc had called him home to deal with the latest crisis. Grabbing her hand, he led them to the common room where Starc would be waiting. It was a surprise to see the room teeming with people, including Prime Hosp's wife.

He knew little about the woman and what he did know, he did not like. She was one of the power hungry wives who basically shopped and did lunch. They spent hours in the communal pathways driving their own agendas. Those women gave nothing back to the community. There were so many Prime spouses who were on different charity boards, earned a living, or found some way to enrich Troyk society. Allaine Hosp was not one of them.

"Tarsea, Solfa had managed to get to Mrs. Hosp before--" He cut him off before Starc could finish his sentence.

Tarsea immediately walked over to Solfa. "Are you out of your mind bringing her to my parents' home?" he yelled and pointed his finger in the direction of the well dressed, shell shocked brunette sitting between his parents.

Solfa stood and went on the offensive. "We did not have a choice. I got to Allaine before anyone else and evacuated her to a safe location where I could talk to her and decide my next steps. We were just about through when our location was compromised. I contacted Starc for assistance. We barely got away and I did not have anywhere else to take her, so I brought her here. Tarsea, Hosp had told her about his meetings with you."

Tarsea looked at Hosp's wife in shock. Hosp had promised he would not tell a soul about their discussions. He directed his next set of questions to the man's widow. "What did he tell you? I want to know everything, including who was involved in what happened yesterday morning."

His mother was just about to get up, when Tarsea stopped her. "Sit, Mother, this is not a social visit." She looked a bit shocked at his outburst, but did as he requested. Neither of his parents communicated to him through the familial pathway regarding his behavior.

It is safe to say Mrs. Hosp looked uncomfortable. "He told me about your discussions, about working toward a peaceful transition. Rance never mentioned any plans for violence to me. He knew I would not have approved, so he met with those people without my knowledge."

Tarsea knew he was not going to get what he wanted out of the woman. It appeared that Solfa had come up with a plan, so he might as well hear her out. "What do you suggest we do next?"

Solfa looked momentary out of sorts, but recovered quickly. "Allaine had several conversations with her husband about other factions interested in peaceful change. I want all their names, so we can investigate who these others are. It may be possible to find people we can leverage going forward. In addition, we may discover who was actually involved in the assassination attempt. If there are any violent conspirators, we will turn them over to The Palace, helping to maintain our covers." Tarsea could not fault Solfa's plan at this point, other than having brought the woman here in the first place.

"We cannot keep her at my parents, we need to find another location to place her until we can get her through the portal." Tarsea wanted her out of the house as soon as they could manage it.

"We can get her to the safe house," Starc suggested. "There was too much activity around the house when I originally met up with Solfa. Things may have quieted down." They had a house on the outskirts of town, not far from the path that led to the portal. It was utilized if they could not immediately make it to the portal due to the presence of people nearby and the threat of communal chatter. He would not be surprised if one of the guys used it to entertain a woman if another location was not available.

"My daughter is at boarding school in a nearby province. I want her with me when I go through the portal." Allaine Hosp said in a determined tone. She still could not look him in the eye.

Tarsea looked at Darden, who shook his head. "Allaine, your daughter is no doubt being watched. We need to get you safely through the portal and your daughter will follow after it is safe."

"That is unacceptable," cried the woman. Her appeal was directed to Solfa. The head of intelligence had the good sense not to respond, merely looked in his direction.

"I am not going to endanger my people for you, Mrs. Hosp. Your daughter is perfectly safe at school. You pull her out, you are endangering her life and the lives of others. If you write her a non-descriptive note, we can make sure she gets it. That is all I can do at this time." Tarsea did not like when people he was saving made demands of him. If this woman had not known of his dealings with her husband, he would have had Solfa take her to The Palace.

It appeared that she took in his words and agreed. She was finally able to look directly at him. "I am sorry for being rude. Rance was supposed to be a peaceful man. My world has fallen apart in the last few days."

"How did you get her here?" Tarsea asked Solfa. It was time to get her the hell out of their home and away from Alex and his parents.

"A blond wig and we pretended to have had a little too much to drink," Starc informed him. He considered what his friend shared. If they faked intoxication to get here, they can leverage that on the way out.

"Starc, can you move her to the safe house alone? Koel will follow you in case there is any trouble. He will take point if you run into any problems. Solfa and Darden, I want you to both stay behind please." Tarsea knew he was close to his anger hitting a breaking point. He had carefully managed his voice purposely not to worry Alexandra.

Solfa helped Mrs. Hosp with the wig and the dark glasses that hid part of her face. While this was going on, Tarsea had a few words with Koel regarding logistics if anything went wrong. Tolfer handed Starc a couple of bottles of fermented keen, as the two left the house.

People were getting re-situated in the common room as Koel left to follow Starc and Mrs. Hosp. Tarsea knew he would be able to breathe a little easier once he got a telepathic confirmation from Starc when they were safe.

Tarsea faced Solfa, his fists clenched at his sides. "Never ever bring a targeted individual to this house again. I will not jeopardize my soul mate or my parents. There is no discussion on this topic."

The woman had the good sense not to say anything, she merely nodded. Tarsea looked at his little pixie to see if she looked angry. Fortunately, she looked fine, but he had to know for sure. *"I hope you are not angry at my dictate."*

"I agree with you. We were blindsided by her presence here. Solfa or Starc should have communicated to you through the warrior's channel and gotten instructions on where to place her. I concur, your parents should not be implicated in any of this. We can talk later about my role going forward." Tarsea smiled, it was more than he had hoped for. He knew she was going to be put in harm's way in the future, but he also knew he would be right alongside her.

"Tarsea," Alexandra said, "I do have a question though. How are you going to get Mrs. Hosp through the portal with patrols monitoring its activity?"

"The portal only has an energy signature on the receiving end when the event horizon opens. We can track when a gateway is opened to our world, not when we open one on this side. They are not physically standing near the gate, although there are regular patrols at the bottom of the trail. A physical presence at the portal may become a reality if we cannot identify the culprits involved in the plot. For now our government is more concerned about who is entering our world."

"Darden," Alexandra appeared to still be struggling with how the portal worked, "how do you know where you are taking Mrs. Hosp?"

"I enter the gateway and through my crystal, I can manipulate the energy signature to open a portal in a particular world. For instance, there is a certain frequency that will open the natural gate in Sedona, Arizona."

"Can the person re-enter a portal they came through?" his soul mate asked.

"Alex," Darden answered, "I am afraid not. The portal closes on the originating side as the last person exits on the arriving side. It is too dangerous to enter the portal on the event horizon side due to the energy emitted."

It appeared his best friend had answered his soul mates questions for now. Tarsea wanted to get the meeting back on track. The sooner he got the answers he wanted, the sooner he could get Alexandra into bed.

"Darden, I want to know what is going on with Benko Jarlyn. His being alive now has to be weighed in the decisions we make going forward." Tarsea knew that eventually he would go through the portal where his soul mate was born and meet with the man himself.

"I met him eight years ago, along with his daughter. Had I not accidentally touched Cassie, I probably would have kept walking and never met the man. We had an immediate connection and the soul mate telepathic channel opened instantaneously.

"You can imagine Benko's reaction when his ten year old daughter had found her soul mate." Darden must have felt Tarsea's mother's intense stare. "I promise, I have been a perfect gentleman, Leenea."

"You better be, young man." His mother had always given Darden a hard time about all the girls he had dated when he was a teenager. When Darden turned eighteen he just stopped dating and his mother had been concerned about his best friend. They had no idea that Darden had stopped going out with women to be faithful to his young soul mate.

"Naturally, from that point on, I visited them as often as I could. There were barriers because of her age, but I was able to watch her grow into the beautiful young woman she is today." Darden smiled, he must have been think-ing of his soul mate. Tarsea did not know if he could have displayed the will-power Darden had shown over all those years.

"The last time I was on Ginkgo Terra, I tried to talk to him through the warrior pathway and succeeded. Benko knows the legend of that pathway and what it means. I sense that eventually he will come back home. His first priority is getting the girls here."

"What girls?" Solfa was a couple days behind in all the excitement that had occurred with Alexandra's arrival.

Tarsea decided he would take over at this point. "The people who went through the portal with Benko passed away. There is an agent in the air that attacks our telepathic brains. They left four girls behind. Most of us found out about this when Alexandra fell through a portal that Darden opened, before it closed."

Solfa shook her head and stared at her cousin. "I guess I was so consumed with the assassination attempt, the warrior channel, and Alexia. It did not dawn on me that she came from another world rather than another province. I had just assumed that some time ago Starta came back with Alexia and placed her in Norri's care. Some intelligence officer I am!"

"I have been working with Benko to bring the girls home. By some miracle Alexandra ended up on the same hiking trail where the natural portal is in Sedona. She was not supposed to be the first one I was to bring over. On my next trip, I will bring her best friend Shirl to our world."

Tarsea squeezed Alexandra's hand. He knew what having Shirl in this world meant to her. From time to time he saw a faraway look in her eyes. He knew she was thinking and worrying about her two friends.

"Everyone," Tarsea said, "we need to see if we can build our network with the people Mrs. Hosp provides. Alex and I should be able to vet them to determine if they are legitimate. I would not be surprised if we get more links into the warrior channel before long. Darden, you need to continue to pressure Benko, we need his commitment. Solfa, anything else I am forgetting."

Her face brightened, Tarsea knew she felt guilty about having brought Mrs. Hosp here and this was his peace offering. "I will interrogate Allaine Hosp."

"Great," Tarsea responded, "when you are done, coordinate with Darden to get her through the portal. You take point on the extraction. Leverage Koel for any logistical planning. He appears to be a happy dolt, but he is an excellent tactical planner."

With those words, Tarsea stood and brought Alexandra up with him. "I am calling it a night. Alexandra has had a long day and I want to take her to bed." He literally dragged her out of the common room as she was wishing everyone a good night.

They had barely stepped into their bedroom when Tarsea was all over Alex. There was a frontal assault on her clothes that were removed before she even caught her breath. The clothes had been so loose fitting, it had not been much of a challenge for Tarsea to remove them.

He lifted her against the door and she wrapped her legs around his waist. She really liked this side of Tarsea, the out of control animal. He snarled and muttered to himself as he held her, kissed her and messed with his leggings to pull himself free. His urgency fed her own.

Tarsea entered her with one powerful thrust. The momentum had such force, her head slammed against the door. *"Sorry,"* he growled and started to carry her to the bed. His foot got caught on the rug and they both went flailing onto the floor. Tarsea took the brunt of the fall, but did not skip a beat in tasting and touching her.

Alex started to laugh as Tarsea continued to make love to her on the rug. She could sense his urgency, evident from the slapstick lovemaking. She utterly adored this man.

He continued to enter and withdraw from her, keeping a constant rhythm she kept pace with. It was over, almost before it began, both climaxing at the same time. "Oh baby, it has been such a long nerve wracking day. I have been holding back for hours."

Gathering her up in his arms, he brought them to the bed. He gently placed her down and laid next to her, bringing Alex into his arms.

"I wanted to be there at The Palace to bring you home and make love to you as soon as we got here. My father said it would be better if I sent my friends. I think he was concerned I would endanger us both if your interview did not go well. Darden, Koel, and Starc had been outside the building just in case."

Alex knew Tarsea would have had some operation related to her safety activated while she was at The Palace. It did not surprise her that his friends were backing him up. Solfa's presence must have really thrown them. She would have loved to listen in on the conversation they were having in the warrior link. Sometime she would have to ask Solfa about what she heard as they walked to the house. In the meantime, she could at least get a response from Tarsea.

"You must have been so happy when I came home with Solfa in tow." She extended the 'so happy' part of the statement. Alex could not help but giggle. Funny, how often she did that. She never considered herself a giggler.

"Let me say my first impulse was to kick her out of the house and grab you." She could tell that sparked something in his mind. He got that frown on his face when he thought too intently. "Who the hell is James Bond? I have been meaning to ask you."

Alex nuzzled his neck and ear. She decided to use their link, since she felt her mouth had better things to do. *"He is a fictional character in a series of books. James Bond is a British Secret Service Agent. They made a bunch of movies from those books. The best James Bond was Sean Connery, but the sexiest is Daniel Craig."* Alex pulled back and gave Tarsea a critical look. "That is who you remind me of, Daniel Craig. It has been driving me crazy trying to figure it out. You are way better looking, but your body type is like his."

"So you like my body?" Tarsea crowed. The man was so full of himself, but he had a reason to be. She loved his body and it was now all hers to enjoy.

"I love every inch of it," she said as she grabbed the tunic he was still wearing and helped him pull it off. Tarsea then got rid of the leggings around his knees at this point.

Tarsea was fully erect again. She rose onto her knees, positioning herself over his stiff rod. Slowly she brought him into her body, torturing her soul mate with each tantalizing inch of him. He had been fast and clumsy, now she was going to be slow and methodical as she made love to him. There was no urgency this time, she had all night.

She could sense he was about to flip her and drive into her again. *"Tarsea, don't you dare change our positions. It is my turn and we are going to go nice and slow. I am going to drive you crazy!"*

He groaned, but he did not attempt to change their positions. He grabbed her waist and held on as she rode him. *"You are ruthless, my little pixie. By The Prime, I love this!"* She could only grin at his reaction to what she was doing to him.

They both came at the same time, Alex experienced the most intense orgasm she had to date. She set that one as the benchmark and would strive to outdo that one each and every night. Yes, she thought, that was an excellent plan.

She collapsed next to him and Tarsea brought her into his arms. Alex knew the topic she was going to bring up was not going to thrill her soul mate.

"About tomorrow," Alex asked, "who are you going to have follow me when I have my date with Raine Narmouth?"

"What makes you think I am going to have you followed?" Tarsea had the gall to look surprised. Alex gave him her 'you can't be serious' look.

"You trust Narmouth as far as you can throw him," Alex told Tarsea. "You are going to have someone with me from the moment I walk out that door."

"You bet your life I am," Tarsea answered. "He so much as touches you, Koel is going to kill him for me."

Alex did not know if he was serious or kidding.

Chapter 20

~

Alex woke feeling groggier than usual. She did not sleep well, due to Tarsea's comment about Koel killing Raine if he so much as touched her, and him waking her up continually to make love. He was insatiable last night.

She rolled out of bed and felt her way to the shower. Her body was sore in places she did not know could get sore. Alex adjusted the shower head so it would provide a needle painful current of water against her aching body.

Tarsea had left out a terrible putty color tunic and legging for her to change into. There was no way she was going to wear that awful outfit, even though she was having lunch with Raine Narmouth. Alex went to the closet and examined the tunics that hung there. She did not want anything that clung to her, but she wanted to wear something that Koel could easily pick her out of a crowd. Today was not the day to blend into the background. She chose a light lavender color tunic and leggings of the same color.

After dressing, she put on the very basics of a light make-up job. She wanted to cover the huge circles under her eyes. Tarsea probably kept her up all night on purpose.

She started walking to the kitchen when there was a knock on the front door. Since she was the closest, she opened the door and there stood Raine Narmouth.

"Hi," Alex welcomed her date, "please, come in. I am running a little late this morning. Would you mind if I had something to drink before we left?"

"No," Raine answered, "please, take your time. I am actually early." She certainly could not fault his manners.

Alex had to admit, Raine was very handsome this morning. He had a dark green tunic on and black leggings. Under different circumstances, she would have been thrilled to go out with him. Although, it was a little weird how often they accidentally kept bumping into each other. On top of everything else, she was sleeping with Tarsea. It felt awkward going on a date with a different man. There was no question she needed to stop second guessing herself and get this over with.

She guided Raine toward the kitchen. There they were greeted by Leenea and Tarsea. Her soul mate did not look happy.

"Raine," Alex said, "I believe you already know Tarsea. This is his mother, Leanea. You met her the other day when you came to see me. I thought I would have a little morning pick me up before we headed for the zoo."

Leenea knew exactly what Alex was asking for. She had no idea what telepathic challenges she would have today in such a public place. A mug of the herbal blend would make it easier to deal with the communal channels.

The room was very quiet as Alex drank her beverage. No one seemed interested in small talk. She was too busy trying to get the herbs down her throat, before she had to leave on a date she never should have made.

"There," Alex said as she finished the drink. "Shall we head on out? Leenea, I will be back in a couple of hours. I know I promised I would help cook dinner tonight."

Tolfer was cooking with Norri assisting. She was just setting the stage to make sure this date would have to be cut short, in case Raine had any ideas to the contrary. She caught a little smile forming on Tarsea's face.

Raine took her hand as soon as they left the house. They started walking in the opposite direction from The Palace and the gathering place she went to last night. He thought she was new to the province, so he would not be surprised when everything she saw was brand new to her.

"Alexia," Raine asked, "how are your headaches? I hope you have fully recovered from your fall."

"I am still getting headaches unfortunately, as well as nosebleeds." How was that for too much information to provide on a date? The more she turned him off the better.

"Poor thing, I understand what you are going through. My head still pounds, although fortunately I have not experienced any nosebleeds." Like

Solfa, he pointed out various Aster Province landmarks as they made their way through the city's streets. There was a cute clothing store, she noted that she wanted to come back to and explore.

They walked for about thirty minutes, talking about nothing in particular. She could see they were approaching the zoo. There were purple azaleas pruned into animal shapes.

"What would you like to do first," Raine asked, "see some animals or eat?" She appreciated that he gave her the choice.

"Actually, I would love to see the giant larma beast you mentioned the other day. My mind was coming up with all sorts of images regarding what the beast looked like. I want to see how close I got."

Raine smiled at her and said, "This way." She turned to see if she could spot Koel. He was nowhere in sight, but she figured he was hanging back out of her and Raine's immediate vision.

They walked past numerous cages, many of the animals she recognized. There were a few that were new to her. She did not want to make it too obvious that she did not know these animals, in case they were indigenous to the Troyk universe.

"Here you go," Raine said, "the famous giant larma beast from the Terra Flora Universe. If you are lucky, I will show you the scar I got capturing the beast." She liked his playful manner. Maybe she would introduce Shirl or Candy to Raine, after they assimilated to this new world and were no longer under a threat of discovery.

Alex looked at the animal. Her wildest imagination was not wild enough to do this beast justice. It truly looked like something out of a horror show, scales and all.

"What does that thing eat?" Alex asked. She hoped it was not small women from the Ginkgo Terra Universe. If she traveled to another universe, she made a note to herself not to go to Terra Flora. She could not imagine facing one of these beasts in the wild.

"It eats a variety of rodents. The animal has an incredibly slow metabolism, so it does not require a lot of food."

"Great!" Alex replied. "On that note, how about lunch. I am game for anything, other than rodents."

Raine laughed and put his arm around Alex and started to guide her toward the zoo's food court. There were a couple of outdoor stalls selling fast food, and what appeared to be three restaurants. They walked into the restaurant closest to the entrance.

The place was bright and colorful. There were pictures of animals everywhere the eye could see. They were on the walls, the lighting fixtures, the ceiling. She did not think she could eat meat in this place. Alex loved a rare steak, but not today.

"Raine, do they have vegetarian items on the menu?" She still needed to be guided related to what to order without giving away the fact she was new to the Troyk universe. Keen was a safe item, but she really would like to try something different.

"You will be glad to know that everything in this restaurant contains no meat. Since there are no fish tanks, they do however have fish and seafood." She had loved shrimp her whole life. They did not serve it often at the orphanage, just on special occasions. To this day, whenever she and her friends went out to celebrate, she had shrimp. She was not sure if they were found in the Troyk universe. They were not on last night's menu.

"Anything that you are having would be great. How about you order for the both of us." He appeared to like her request. Some men like to order for women.

The waiter came and Raine ordered telepathically, as Tarsea did the night before. Almost immediately an iced herbal beverage was delivered to her. He was served what looked like to be some kind of ale.

Their entrees were served shortly after their drinks. The dish smelled wonderful and it tasted like heaven. It contained a variety of seafood, including shrimp. Naturally, it was served on a bed of keen.

"Wow," Alex said, "thank you for ordering and taking me to the zoo. This is perfect."

She never believed in eating like a bird, even on the few dates she had. He watched her eat and had the same look of satisfaction that Tarsea had on his face when she ate. She guessed it went back to the Stone Age, when men hunted to feed their women.

They both finished their meals and drinks in record time. Raine paid the bill and they were back looking at the animals.

She was having such a good time, she had not noticed they had headed down a walkway isolated from the rest of the park. Alex stopped and tried to see where they were going.

"Sweetheart," Raine said, "there is an exhibit back there you have to see."

First off, she did not like him calling her sweetheart. Secondly, she did not like being on this unpopulated path. "I do not think so, Raine. On first dates I like to be surrounded by people, no offense. A girl cannot be too careful. Things have been great until now, please do not ruin it."

"Alexia, I want to taste you. Ever since I saw you at The Childers', I have not been able to think about anything but you."

He picked her up and started carrying her deeper into the walkway. She started fighting him, but it did no good. It was time to play dirty, she started to claw at his face with her nails. Raine put her down and smacked her face. She was just about to knee him in his jewels, when Koel and Tolfer showed up.

"I have you, Alex," Tolfer comforted her. "I am getting you out of here. We should have gotten to you earlier. Somehow we missed him bringing you down this walkway."

She walked with Tolfer in a semi daze. He brought her to a bench in the main part of the zoo. Koel had not made it back to join them yet. Alex was wondering if he was really going to kill Raine. She did not want to think if she wanted him dead or not. Thank God they got to her in time.

It was probably only a couple of minutes, but it felt like an eternity before Koel joined them. He did not say anything, he just patted Tolfer on the back and they were on their way. She did not have the courage to ask Koel what condition he left Raine in. All she wanted was to get home and take a scalding hot shower. The water would wash away his touch and his scent.

Tarsea paced the common room like a caged animal. Alexandra had been back for an hour and she was still cloistered in their room. His mother and her aunt were with his soul mate. He understood this was a time for women and the presence of a male was not wanted.

When Tolfer contacted him that Alexandra had been attacked by that low life scum, he wanted to kill the bastard. He understood that Koel had done a pretty good job of messing him up. His first reaction was to meet them on their way back to the house. Tolfer warned him back, that he would only upset Alexandra and make a public scene.

"How did you both miss him taking her into an isolated area?" Tarsea asked. He kicked himself mentally for not being with them and protecting Alexandra. It was his responsibility.

"I have asked myself that question over and over again, Tarsea," Tolfer said. "I still have not figured it out. We were probably fifty feet behind them when we turned the corner and they were gone. Unfortunately, I underestimated the man and what he was capable of doing. I am so sorry."

"Tarsea," Koel spoke up for the first time, "she is too independent. She did not scream or leverage the communal pathway. When we got to them she had scratched his face and was about to kick him in the balls."

"Fortunately," Tolfer added, "he did not hit her too hard. If that even makes any sense. What kind of man hits a woman, anyway? I do not think she will even bruise. When we got to them, he was in worse shape than she was in. If we had been a few seconds slower, she would have had him on his knees. For such a small woman, she is certainly fierce." The fact that Alexandra had been able to partially defend herself did not lessen the guilt he was feeling. He swore the next time he saw Narmouth, Tarsea was going to kill him. The man had hit his little pixie.

"Well, this ends her dating and intelligence career." Tarsea did not think he could go through another afternoon like this one. Hopefully, this experience will have put a damper on the allure of being a spy in her mind.

"Tarsea," his mother said, "she is asking for you. I think she will want to stay in your room for the rest of today. In a couple of hours, I will bring you both something to eat."

He headed for his room. None of his girlfriends had ever been attacked, he was not quite sure how to act once he was in their room with her. Tarsea was just going to have to follow whatever signs and direction Alexandra gave him. Guilt continued to consume him that he did not properly protect her.

When he got to his room, he knocked and then entered. She had changed into a cushy robe, all bundled up. She was sitting on the bed and Norri was by her side. She kissed her niece and left the room.

"Alex," he softly said, "how are you doing?"

"He was so nice, Tarsea. I did not see it coming until it was too late." She looked so vulnerable. He knew she was going over this afternoon over and over again in her head.

"It sounds like you got the best of him though. Tolfer said he looked a lot worse than you did." Her cheek was a little red, but other than that, he could not tell she had just been attacked. He knew it took more of a psychological toll on her than a physical one.

"Candy made sure we took self-defense classes. She tailored moves just for me, due to my size. These are lethal weapons." Alex raised her hand and showed him her nails. Although it was probably an incorrect thought, he had felt those nails on his back a time or two.

"Remind me to thank Candy when I finally meet her. She protected you better than I did. No more dating Alex, or at least let me set you up with cover dates with men I trust."

"I know I should have listened to you, Tarsea. Even Solfa warned me off him." Alex looked a little spooked, he guessed she had not meant to mention that little tidbit. He was going to let it rest for now.

He knew Alexandra well enough to know she was holding back on asking him another question. She kept looking at him and then dropped her eyes. "Is there something else you wanted to ask me? You know you can ask me anything."

She seemed to be struggling with herself related to either what to ask or how to ask it. "Tarsea, if Raine had been a mind control telepath, could he have forced me to willingly have sex with him this afternoon, if I had not been immune to their compulsions?"

Tarsea stared at his soul mate. He had not expected that question and had to consider how to answer her. So little was really known about the extent of mind control telepathic ability to manipulate what would ordinarily be considered rape. He owed her an answer, regardless of how awkward his explanation was going to be.

"A mind control telepath cannot force anyone to do something contrary to their beliefs or how someone is wired. If someone is married or in a committed relationship and would not consider having sex with anyone else, a mind control telepath cannot convince them to have sex. However, if there is just the slightest bit of interest, they can manipulate that grain of interest into a strong sexual desire."

Alexandra considered his words for several minutes. "What if there was at one point some interest, but the woman starts fighting before he uses mind control. Can he manipulate the woman then?"

"Alex, to be perfectly honest, I do not know. Mind control advocates focus on political and economic power. There has been little discussion or court cases related to mind control and rape."

Alex's face contorted in horror as she ingested the information. "Oh God! It is rape of both the mind and the body. How can you live in this world?"

There was so much of his world he had worked to shelter her from. He wanted her safe and managing the numerous telepathic channels before he shared the true reality of his world with her. A world he worked to change.

"Alex, we have been secretly working to eliminate mind control from our political and professional lives. What we are talking about is certainly not condoned and near to impossible to prove. Even after we succeed, a small percentage of our population will still try to manipulate others for their own gain. I have to believe that even today people are basically ethical and have some degree of morals. There should be a certain decency related to how a man treats a woman, regardless of his telepathic abilities."

What he said must have resonated in Alexandra's mind, because she smiled and kissed his cheek. "Thank you, Tarsea. I know that was probably not easy for you to explain to me. Even in my world, atrocities occur. Like you, I have to believe that mankind is basically good. Otherwise, I don't know how any of us could function with all the bad in the world."

"I do not want to appear to be bowing out of this discussion. When you are ready, I am sure Solfa or Tarah could give their insight that I do not have on the subject."

Alexandra yet again smiled at him, lighting up her face. "That is actually an excellent idea! Violence against women seems to be a problem in both our worlds. I will ultimately have the discussion with them. I am sure when Shirl and Candy are here, they will want to join in. It is another cause to add to my ever growing list of things that need to change in this world. Solfa is high in the government, maybe it's something we can work on even before we have a leadership change. I could not imagine that even Jeryl Jarlyn condones women being victims of mind control to perform sexual acts."

He had been leaning on his dresser as they had their discussion. Alexandra shifted from sitting to lying on the bed. She patted the empty side of the mattress beside her. Tarsea slipped out of his shoes and joined his soul mate. He took her in his arms and held her.

Alex drifted to sleep soon after. It was not surprising after he kept her up most of the night and the day she just experienced. Guilt once again consumed him. She must have been exhausted when she was with Narmouth, not in full control of all her faculties. Yet again he had considered his own needs, not what had been best for his soul mate. He thought of his reaction to her going into intelligence, not what it would mean to Alexandra. He had failed her on so many levels.

After about an hour she stirred in his arms. Unlike the morning, Alex woke alert from her nap.

"Can I get you anything? Some herbal beverage or chocolate? My mom will be preparing a dinner tray for us in about an hour."

Her eyes got big as soon as he mentioned chocolate. Alexandra started to laugh, it was music to his ears.

"No, thank you. I want to talk about tomorrow and my lunch with Charzilla and her friends."

"You are not serious, you are still going through with that lunch date?" He had no idea who Charzilla was, but he was certain she was referring to Chartail. Alexandra had been calling her all sorts of colorful names. With everything that happened today, he just assumed she would lay low for a couple of days.

"I am not going to let Raine impact my life any more than he already has. Besides, it's only lunch with three women. Even if one of the women is a venomous wraith, who is set on seeking her revenge on you."

Tarsea just shook his head. "Alex, where do you get this stuff?"

"A lot of Friday and Saturday nights at home watching bad movies. Anyway, I need to know about them and you have to tell me." His little pixie was back. Her chin was raised and she had determination written all over her face.

Tarsea sighed, giving in to her desire to have this conversation. "Unlike her father, Chartail is not a mind control telepath. None of her friends or my former girlfriends that she will drag along with her are either. They are rather shallow, otherwise they probably would not have dated me."

"Wow, remind me not to ask you to describe me." Alex was just kidding, but she could tell from Tarsea's expression, he took her seriously.

"Alex, you are smart, intelligent, and funny. You have committed yourself to making our world better, after having only been in Aster Province for just days."

Alex leaned in and kissed his lips. He took his tongue and licked his wet lips, bringing her taste into his mouth.

"Was that all right, Alex?" He kissed her without taking into account whether the physical contact was welcome after her experience this afternoon.

"I liked that, I always do. That sorry excuse for a man is not going to mess up what we have together. Although, I would rather not make love tonight. I'd rather have you hold me and we can talk."

"That is fine with me, baby. What else do you want to talk about?"

"We are not done talking about tomorrow and my lunch with the girls. This is important, Tarsea, she used to be your cover. Now she is going to be mine."

"Fine, I will walk you over there tomorrow. There is some shopping I want to do while you are having lunch with them."

"Shopping?" Tarsea could see this was a topic she was very interested in. He could not wait to shop for more clothes, furniture, dishes, and everything they would ultimately need for their new life together.

"Yes," Tarsea said "there are a couple of things I want to pick up. I am not saying anything more."

"Not fair," Alex cried, "don't I get a hint or anything?"

He shook his head and that was the end of that.

"Well, then I want to get back to discussing Chartail and her friends. I want to make sure I have all the ammunition I need for tomorrow to come out the victor. By the way, Tarsea, no more putty or gross colored tunic purchases for me."

Tarsea chuckled. That horrible colored tunic was a purchase he made at a thrift shop. He did not like the idea of other men looking at his little pixie. When she had lunch with the girls tomorrow, however, he wanted her to look great. He almost felt sorry for Chartail and her friends. Alexandra was a force to be reckoned with. Those women were not going to know what hit them.

Chapter 21

Alex woke up slowly as usual. The bed next to her was cold. She really wished Tarsea was not an early riser. It would have been wonderful to snuggle with him as she slowly came back to the land of the living. Oh crap! She was having lunch with the evil one and her heinous cohorts today.

She reluctantly rolled out of the safety of the bed. Memories of Raine Narmouth came back to her. Alex knew she was going to have to leave the house. She was still apprehensive about it, regardless of what she had told Tarsea last night. He held her throughout the night, not attempting anything amorous, other than chaste kisses.

Somehow she made it to the shower. Alex loved to start the day with the purple floral enhanced shampoo. The shampoo's essence filled the stall, her nose having its own orgasm as she breathed in the aroma. Slowly, Alex worked the conditioner through her hair. It had the same scent, just not as poignant. Leenea added a bottle of conditioner yesterday morning to her toiletries. Both women laughed over the lack of grooming men did, compared to women.

Tarsea had left out the lavender and gray tunic she had worn when they had dinner together. That dinner date seemed like a million years ago. She slipped the tunic over her head and put on the leggings.

Alex stood in front of the mirror, trying to figure out what she wanted to do with her hair. She ended up just clipping back her bangs, keeping them out of her face. Her mind waffled whether to put on make-up. Having seen Chartail, she decided against it. In the end, she just put on some lip gloss. Lip gloss was a requirement in Phoenix because it was so dry. It had become second nature to wear it every morning.

Satisfied with how she looked, she slipped on her shoes and made her way to the kitchen. She had to leave in an hour to meet Chartail, so she was not going to eat anything. Some of that herbal tea would be a perfect way to start her day. It may reduce some of the anxiety she was having in leaving the house.

There were voices coming from the common room, so she decided to go there first. Odds were there was a pot of tea on one of the tables.

As she entered, the room got quiet. Oh God, what now? There was a woman she had never seen sitting next to Solfa. The woman took one look at her and started to cry. She immediately got up and ran to Alex, throwing her arms around her.

"Alexia," Solfa provided the introduction, "this is my mother. She is your mother's cousin." It now made sense why this woman was crying and holding her like she would never let her go.

"You look so much like your mother, Alexia. She was quite a bit younger than I was, but there was something about Starta I always loved. I was devastated when she left with your father. She should have done what the rest of us did and just accepted things. She would still be alive if she had."

Alex held the woman as she cried. A sorrow so deep, she was not sure how to comfort her.

"Can she be trusted?" she asked Tarsea. It was true this woman loved her mother, but she could also present a risk to everyone in the room.

"Solfa told me that her mother has been very bitter about what happened. She is also aware of what her daughter has been up to. This is the last person that will put you at risk." Hearing what Tarsea communicated made Alex relax a little bit.

She felt the need to comfort this woman who loved her mother so much. A sharp mental pain hit Alex as she once again felt the loss of the mother she never knew.

"I am not going anywhere," Alex said softly. "I promise. Solfa told me you are her mother, but not what your name is."

"My name is Pattrice. I loved your mother so much, I am truly blessed to have her daughter back. When Solfa told me Norri was here, I wanted to come over immediately. She held me off until this morning and then I found out about you. I cannot believe I am holding Starta's daughter in my arms." The poor woman started crying all over again.

Alex caught her aunt's eye and mouthed, "Please, help me."

Norri got up and took Pattrice back to where she had been sitting. She had her arm around her cousin and was speaking softly, comforting her.

"Good morning," Tarsea whispered in her ear after he walked over and joined her. He gave her a loving kiss on her forehead and a gentle hug.

Leenea was right behind him with a steaming cup of herbs for her. She took the mug and kissed her on the cheek. Alex grew even closer to this wonderful woman after she sat and talked with her yesterday afternoon.

Tarsea led her over to the couch, both ready to join the discussion. Alex noticed that he was the only male in the room. *"Where is everyone else?"*

He smiled and brought his arm around her shoulder. *"There were too many women, so my dad and Tolfer went out for breakfast. Tolfer has to teach this afternoon and my dad will attend the Prime Council meeting to hear what is being discussed."*

She looked toward Solfa and was curious where they stood on the events from yesterday. Her world recently had revolved around the episode with Narmouth. *"Did they finish interviewing Mrs. Hosp and get her through the portal?"* Once again talking to Tarsea using their private channel.

Tarsea responded, *"Early this morning, before the sun rose. We got some additional names, we will chat this afternoon or tomorrow about our next steps. Enjoy time with your newly discovered family."*

Alex went back to sipping the herbal drink after telepathically conversing with Tarsea. She watched her aunt continue to try and calm her cousin. Emotions were running high. It still blew her away that she had gone from being an orphan to discovering this wonderful extended family she had in a parallel world. From time to time she even pinched herself to make sure she was not dreaming.

Pattrice seemed to have gotten control of herself once again. "Norri is going to be moving in with me until the apartment is ready. I would like you to join us. There is plenty of room. It will give us all a chance to get to know each other."

Alex stared at her cousin's mother. She was not sure what to do. When she first came to this house, she knew it was temporary. However, that was before she found out Tarsea was her soul mate. There was no question she liked sharing a bed with him and had planned to continue doing so.

Tarsea stood up cleared his throat. "I would like to make an announcement, or rather, I would like to ask Alexia a question." He then got down on one knee and took her hand. "Alexia, will you marry me?"

Alex was overwhelmed and she struggled to catch her breath. She wondered, yet again, what was the man thinking? No, no, no, he did not just ask her to marry him, did he?

"What! My aunt asks me to move in with her and now you are asking me to marry you in front of everyone? Overreact much?"

"I was going to buy you a ring this afternoon and ask you tonight when we were alone. Remember, I mentioned I had some shopping to do today."

"Well, crap, I'm so sorry, Tarsea. I am sure it would have been beautiful and my cousin messed up your plans."

"Alex, are you going to answer me? Everyone is looking at us."

She looked around and noticed all eyes were looking at her expectantly. How long had she and Tarsea been conversing through the soul mate channel? She thought she should answer him and end the suspense. Her mind was spinning. She was conflicted over how to answer him. Time, she needed time to figure out what to do.

"Tarsea, I would be honored to eventually marry you. We have only known each other for a grand total of six days. You just broke up with a woman that the world knows you dated for seven months. Our existence and safety is dependent on appearances."

He looked like a wounded puppy. She really wished that he had not asked her in front of everyone. It killed her she had to temporarily turn him down with an audience present.

"Son," Leenea addressed Tarsea, "your father and I pretended to have a moderate dating period and then a fairly quick wedding. Alex is right, yet again showing wisdom beyond her years."

"I can move in with Norri and Pattrice for a short while, for appearances sake. We can have date night and sleepovers at your place, just like a normal couple. Then I can move in with you and we can eventually get married. I want Shirl and Candy there. We have to get them here so they can help me plan the wedding."

He still did not look happy. She really did not understand what the rush was. With his reputation, who would believe they were engaged anyway. Tarsea had given every indication that he was committed to her. She still wanted to soothe his bruised ego.

"Tarsea, you grew up with the legend of soul mates. Maybe a lot of what you are feeling for me is related to that, rather than organic feelings. I did not grow up with those stories. There is no question I have very strong feelings for you. Let's continue to get to know each other."

"I was really looking forward to getting you a ring this afternoon and putting it on your finger. That ring would symbolize that you are mine."

"Hey," Alex announced to the world, "I'm not averse to getting jewelry! We can still go shopping for a ring, just not an engagement ring. Maybe an Irish Claddagh ring. Do you have them here?"

"What is it?" Tarsea asked.

"The ring has two hands clasping a heart. The hands symbolize friendship and the heart symbolizes love. If I wear the ring facing in, it means I am taken. I remember when Angel gave Buffy her Claddagh ring and then he turned evil." She still missed that damn television show.

Tarsea smiled, "I have no idea what you are talking about. But, we can see what the jeweler has."

Alex figured they could go after she had lunch with the Gorgon sisters. Medusa had nothing on Chartail as far as she was concerned.

"Guess we should be going to meet the ladies for lunch. If I had known we would be having a family reunion and a proposal, I certainly would not have made this lunch appointment. Since I just met Chartail, it would be rude to cancel on her." Alexandra knew she could leverage Tarsea's former girlfriend and did not want to alienate her from the beginning.

Regardless of the attack, she still planned on becoming an intelligence officer. It meant too much to her to let the slime ball ruin her plans. She figured this lunch was her first step down that road. Buckle up, she was ready to go.

Chapter 22

Alex stood in front of the restaurant where she was going to have lunch with Chartail and two of her friends. Tarsea had just dropped her off and was supposedly going shopping. She had a feeling that he or one of his friends was hanging around in case of any trouble. The incident yesterday with Raine Narmouth had not only spooked her, but the men in her life as well. In the past, she only had Shirl and Candy. Now she had her family, Tarsea, his family and friends.

Taking a deep breath, she walked into the restaurant. She knew she had to give off the aura of self-confidence if she was going to survive in these shark infested waters. Fortunately, it was still early, the place was relatively empty. It was not difficult to find Chartail. Today the she-beast was wearing a bright fuchsia blouse.

Alex navigated around tables covered with white tablecloths. Each table was set with ivory and gray colored plates, accompanied by wine glasses and water goblets. Things were not so different from home in this respect. It was only the telepathic ordering of your meal that was so dissimilar. That was going to take some getting used to.

Chartail got up and waved when she spotted her. Alex was surprised by the jovial welcome. The woman seemed genuinely pleased to see her. She started to feel bad about all the terrible names she had been calling Chartail in her mind.

As Alex neared the table, Chartail came over and gave her the same fake kisses on both sides of her face as she did two nights ago. "I am so pleased you were able to join us. Please sit and I will introduce you to everyone."

Alex took the only available chair, the one right next to Chartail.

"I am Sondra," the blond woman to her left said as she grabbed her hand. "It is so nice to meet you. I dated Tarsea right before he started dating Jessalyn." She indicated to the woman across from Alex, another beautiful tall blonde. Chartail was right, she really was not Tarsea's type.

"Wow!" that was all Alex could think to say. How many women had Tarsea dated? She took a big gulp of water. If there were menus she could have started looking at one. She was forced to look at her three lovely lunch companions. Why weren't there any menus?

"Please," Jessalyn said, "do not feel awkward. We have all been where you are now. Tarsea is a great boyfriend, while it lasts."

Alex figured her discomfort had been written all over her face. So much for ruling the situation and coming out on top. These women scared her to death. Soul mate or not, how was she going to compete for Tarsea when these are the women he had been dating in the past?

"Honey," Sondra joined the conversation, "we are here for you when the inevitable happens. We are sort of like a club. Admittance is being dumped by Tarsea Childers. I guess we could say you are in the initiation phase, you are actually still dating him."

She took a momentary break from the conversation and listened into the communal channels. There were various comments about the beautiful three blondes at the table. Alex was not surprised. For once she was happy to be invisible to many people's eyes.

"Alex," Chartail added after visually examining her for several minutes, "we have to take you shopping. We need to add some color into your wardrobe. You kind of blend into the background."

She could not fault Chartail's observation. There were times she did need to stand out of the shadows and needed to get some nicer clothes. At home, she went shopping with Shirl. Alex had never been into clothes, so her best friend usually directed what she bought and wore. Shirl was always going on about what colors she should wear. She could not remember what colors she said were best for her light auburn hair and her coloring. Now Chartail was offering to help her select clothing. Under different circumstances she could see Chartail and her becoming friends.

"That would be very nice of you, Chartail. I only brought a couple of outfits with me and do not know the stores here." Alex all of a sudden thought of that cute clothing store she passed when she was with Raine. She wondered if she was ever going to be able to stomach going there after all.

The waiter came with the menus. Since this was the first time ordering off the lunch menu, the three women ordered first. As they telepathically made their selections, Alex looked at the menu to see what they were ordering. Two of the three ordered the house special salad, she felt that was her best bet. When in Rome, after all.

Alex placed her order telepathically. She included a glass of the wine she had last night with Tarsea. As she was handing her menu to the waiter, their drinks arrived. You've got to love the efficiency of this place.

She took a sip of her wine and concentrated on Jessalyn to see if she could read her mind. The woman was talking about the store where she had purchased her bright red blouse and what a great deal she got.

Alex felt a weird kind of static and then picked up, *"I really paid a lot more for the blouse, but they do not need to know that."* She choked on her wine, placing the glass down, as she continued to cough. The shopping conversation ceased as the women asked if she was all right. Alex nodded as she got the coughing under control.

Once again Alex leveraged the soul mate link to share her accomplishment with him. *"I did it, Tarsea, I was able to read someone's thoughts!"*

"That is great, baby! Enjoy your lunch. Do not over stress your brain with your new talent." Alexandra was touched by Tarsea's concern. She decided she'd have more herbs when she got home so he would not worry. Besides, the last thing she wanted was another nose bleed. She was going to become anemic if they continued. Eating liver to increase her iron count was a horrifying thought.

The waiter came with a bread basket. Alex grabbed a roll and what she thought was flavored butter to spread on it. She took a bite and yet again was blown away about how good food was in the Troyk Universe. Maybe her taste buds had been impacted by the portal.

"Yum!" Alex shared with the group. "This is really delicious. You have much better restaurants here than where I am from." It was the truth after all. She just did not mention where exactly she was from.

Sondra concurred, "The Aster Province is known for their restaurants and excellent wines. This one has their own bread and pastry chef."

Alex continued to nibble on the bread as the women talked about what their favorite restaurants were. She would have to share the information with Tarsea. While she listened, she concentrated on Sondra.

The woman smiled at Alex, thinking she was captivated by what she was saying. *"I have to fast every time I go out to dinner. My new desk job is causing me to put on weight."*

Alex was amazed how easy it was to pick up that thought. There was no static or any pressure on her brain.

Chartial's dish arrived and their salads. The dressing came on the side. Alex placed her fork in the bowl and tasted the dressing. Not surprising, it was delicious. She poured the dressing on the salad and she started to attack her lunch.

"How is your salad, Alexia?" Chartail asked as she was digging into her keen and some kind of mushroom dish.

"Everything is so good. I am going to put on a ton of weight living here." She could not believe how comfortable she was with these ladies. Alex felt a little guilty about reading their minds.

"So," Chartail said, "you have decided to move here and live with your aunt?"

"Yes," Alex replied between bites of her salad, "that is the plan."

"Do not worry, Alexia. You are slim, you can afford to put on some weight." She was liking Sondra more and more.

Everyone was enjoying their lunches and the conversation temporarily stopped as they ate. Alex decided she would try to read Chartail's mind. Guilt was overruled by her need to practice her new skill. She was also curious if Chartail's inner thoughts mirrored her friendly exterior.

She concentrated on the woman next to her. The woman who Tarsea had sex with, but never shared his bed. She was getting the same strange static, but still could not pick up a train of thought. Maybe she was so busy eating, she was not thinking about anything specific.

Her concentration was broken when she heard a man's voice.

"Hello, Alexia."

She looked up to see Raine Narmouth staring at her. His face was a collection of black, blue and purple bruises and the scratches she inflicted. Koel did a real number on him, deservedly.

"Raine!" Alex cried, "What are you doing here? After you attacked me yesterday, I thought you got the message I was off limits."

The three women at the table were watching the exchange. Chartail started to get a very hostile expression on her face.

"Alexia," Raine pleaded, "it was all a misunderstanding. I did not mean to hit you, I was just trying to calm you down."

"I am sorry, but picking me up and dragging me into an isolated location would panic anyone. You need to stay away from me."

Chartail stood and addressed Raine. "You need to get out of here before I call the authorities. My father is Prime Adholm and he can ruin your career."

Just as Chartail finished talking, the restaurant's manager came up and physically escorted Raine Narmouth off the premises.

As he was being evicted from the restaurant, Raine was shouting out to her. "Alexia, you need to forgive me. Please, give me another chance."

"That was really creepy," Jessalyn said. "What happened yesterday?"

"I was on a date with him and we were having a great time. The next thing I know, he is dragging me down an isolated walkway. Fortunately, Koel and Tolfer rescued me. They have kind of adopted me as a kid sister. Can you believe, they followed me to the zoo? They did not like that I was dating Raine, there is some kind of bad blood between them."

"Thank the Supreme Being they were there," Sondra commented. "They were probably looking out for Tarsea's interests, since you are currently dating him."

The manager of the restaurant came by with another round of drinks for the table. "Please accept my apologies that confrontation happened in our restaurant. Your lunch is on the house."

"Thank you," Alex said, "that is very sweet of you." She was grateful for the second glass of wine after the encounter with Raine.

Things calmed down and all four women started to pick at their remaining lunch. Everyone seemed to have lost their appetites.

She decided she needed to distract her mind away from the latest episode with Raine Narmouth. After taking another bite, she concentrated on Chartail. The woman had really backed her up this afternoon. All she got was static once again.

Alex was just about to give up, when she picked something up. "*I better stop eating, I have to meet Stephano this evening for dinner here. He really messed things up with Prime Hosp and the assassination attempt. All my hard work and what did I get, nothing!*"

All she could do was stare at Chartail. She needed to get a grip on things and not give herself away. Alex took another sip of wine, a bite of her salad and looked at Sondra.

She was really torn about what to do. Chartail was part of the assassination plot, yet she just helped her get rid of Raine Narmouth. Two men were dead, she could not ignore what she just heard. The welfare of the Aster Province has to be her first priority, regardless of her personal feelings.

"Tarsea, we are going to have to cancel shopping for now. I know who was behind the assassination attack. We need to regroup at your parents' house. Come and pick me up in about twenty minutes."

"Alex, do not do anything stupid. Finish your lunch and then meet me in front of the trail we walked on yesterday. It is not far from the entrance to the restaurant. I am heading over there now."

"There is something else you need to know. Raine Narmouth came up to me in the restaurant. Chartail and the restaurant's manager took care of the situation for now. Tarsea, he is not going to just go away I am afraid. Let me finish things here with the girls and meet you."

Fortunately Tarsea did not respond to her. It would have only resulted in delaying her executing an exit strategy and meeting up with him. She figured they were going to have a lot of words on the subject.

"What do you girls do for exercise? I figure with all this great food, I am going to have to get more physical activity in." Alex pushed back her salad bowl. She needed to get out of here gracefully.

"We all belong to the same gym. They have great classes. This was fun, how about the four of us getting together again for lunch this time next week," Jessalyn suggested.

"I would love that. When Chartail suggested we have lunch together, I have to admit, I was apprehensive. You three are wonderful and I had a great time. I was afraid if I moved here, I would not know anyone." Alex was not sure if she was going to be able to continue the relationship with the other two women once Chartail was arrested.

"It is not your fault Tarsea goes through women like someone with an allergy attack goes through tissue." Alex could not help herself, she laughed at Jessalyn's comment.

"On that note, I need to leave. I am looking forward to seeing you all next week." Alex got up from the table and started walking toward the restaurant's park entrance.

She never wanted to get out of anywhere faster than she wanted to leave the restaurant and get to Tarsea. Alex headed for the trail and spotted him almost immediately.

He opened his arms as she started running toward him. She felt his arms entwine around her and she felt safe again. Raising her head, she kissed him.

"I want to go home," Alex shared with Tarsea. They had to deal with Raine Narmouth and figure out what to do about Chartail.

Chapter 23

~

Tarsea walked the streets of Aster Province with his arm across his soul mate's shoulder. She seemed visibly shaken by what happened at lunch. He held off asking her about Narmouth or who was behind the assassination attempt. He figured she would tell him when she was ready or was waiting to tell the group at one time.

After Alex had communicated to him that she knew who was behind the attack on Jeryl Jarlyn, he put out an alert through the warrior link that new information had been discovered. Everyone available was making their way to his parents' home. After he sent out the broadcast, Alex then told him about another incident with Narmouth. They were going to have to do something about the guy.

He should have kept an eye on the restaurant. After the beating Koel gave Narmouth, Tarsea had assumed the man would have the sense to give Alex a wide berth. It appeared he had some kind of obsession toward his soul mate. He would make sure that someone watched her every time she left the house.

They reached their destination, just as Darden and Solfa arrived. Tarsea greeted his best friend, while Alex hugged her cousin. Alexandra still did not seem eager to share the information she had uncovered.

His mother let them in, with concern in her eyes for Alexandra. "Would you like a mug of herbal tea, dear? I know you have just had lunch, but it may help. You look a little pale."

Tarsea looked at his little pixie. His mother was right, she did appear a little pale. Alex had been a little flushed in the park from running. He wondered if it was the information she uncovered or Narmouth that upset her the most. The combination of both must be overwhelming her.

"That would be lovely, Leenea. I had never read anyone's mind before. I guess it took more out of me than I thought." Alexandra sounded exhausted. Tarsea led her into the common room and the two of them sat in the lone love seat.

Within ten minutes everyone except Tolfer was present and ready to hear Alexandra's report.

"Before we start discussing the assassination attempt, I want to talk about what we can do about Raine Narmouth. He approached Alex at the restaurant."

"He was not involved in the plot, was he?" questioned Starc. There was a hopeful tone to his question. Tarsea knew there was bad blood between his friend and Narmouth. He had his suspicions about what caused the issue, but never pressed Starc about it.

"I wish," Alex answered, "that would have killed two birds with one stone. Life is never that easy. What are our options?"

"Unfortunately," Darden said, "there is not a lot we can do. We cannot report it to the authorities. Alex does not exist in this world. It would place unwanted scrutiny on her."

"It gets worse," Starc shared. "The bastard is also too highly placed in the Crystal Telepath Guard. I just found out this morning that I will be reporting to him. He cannot just disappear. Nothing would make me happier than having Darden send him to some hell hole of a world."

For once in his life he considered leveraging a mind control telepath to take care of the problem. He knew that Tarah could compel him to leave Alexandra alone. It was a true reflection of his feelings for her that he would consider using a practice he had worked his whole life to abolish. Tarsea decided to hold off on that alternative for now. He had to come to grips with his feelings for her and his commitment to the cause. His opinion had always been that any type of mind control was wrong. Where did you draw the line over what was acceptable and what was a violation of someone's mind?

"So," Tarsea conceded, "there is nothing we can do for the time being. We just have to make sure Alex is shadowed by one of us whenever she leaves the house. You also need to hold off on moving in with Norri for the time being."

Alex nodded. He was relieved she readily agreed to his dictate on that subject. It was a testament to how much Narmouth had spooked her. She also did not complain about having someone following her at all times.

"When Alex is working for me," Solfa joined in the conversation, "I will make sure she has added protection. I do not have to explain why, I will just double the protection we provide our operatives."

Tarsea turned to Starc. "Can you watch him at work? Look for anything you can to discredit him."

Starc nodded. He knew that Starc would relish the opportunity to discredit Narmouth. Going forward, he would try to pair Starc and Alexandra together when he needed someone to follow his soul mate.

"All right, Alex," Tarsea asked, "what did you hear during lunch about the assassination plot?" He was ready to move the group on to the next subject, the reason why they were together this afternoon.

Tarsea took her hand, knowing she was upset. Her coloring still had not returned to normal.

Alex looked stunned. She shook her head and appeared to be struggling over what to say. "I was expecting to hear about shopping, boys, and dieting. The last thing I expected, right out the gate, was a confession."

Solfa sat on the table in front of her cousin. "Alexia, tell us what you heard. All my intelligence officers have a hard time with their first debrief. Some feel they are being disloyal or breaking a confidence."

Alex took a sip from her mug, Tarsea could see she was visibly shaking. It was almost as if she did not want to identify who was responsible, but could not figure out why. She looked up at her cousin, with unshed tears in her eyes. It was tearing Tarsea apart.

"I first listened to Sondra and Jessalyn's thoughts. Then I concentrated on Chartail. I heard she was meeting some guy named Stephano for dinner and how he messed things up with Prime Hosp. She thought about all the work she had done resulting in nothing."

Everyone in the room was shocked, Tarsea most of all. He had slept with the woman, dated her for seven months. There were several occasions she was on his arm when he met Prime Hosp at a social event. Never for one minute had he suspected of her plotting behind everyone's backs to assassinate the Prime Ruler.

"Boy," the silence was broken when Koel said, "I was not expecting that! Tarsea, guess she does not talk in her sleep." Leave it to Koel to make a snide remark related to this news, he was going to kill him.

Tarsea was about to rip him to shreds when Alex started to laugh. She got up and went to kiss Koel on the cheek.

"God," Alex exclaimed, "I needed that. I love you, Koel. Never change. You always put things in perspective with that smart mouth of yours." Koel put one of those goofy smiles on his face.

Tarsea felt he must be feeling more secure in his relationship with his soul mate. Had Alex kissed Koel just a few days before, he probably would have killed his friend. It seemed natural now for her to feel for his friends and family as he did.

Solfa brought everyone back to the discussion about what Alexandra heard. "Does anyone know who this Stephano could be? Tarsea, was there any indication that she was upset with her father or the government?"

Tarsea shook his head. "I am as surprised as everyone else. Chartail is the last person I would have pegged as the mastermind of an assassination plot. She always appeared so shallow. So much for appearances. I guess I never really knew her."

Alex started laughing again. "Were they going to outlaw bright colors?" Tarsea knew her laughter was relieving the stress she had bottled up. Alex lifted her hand, indicating to the group, she was getting herself under control.

His soul mate seemed to have gotten over her giggles. "I am so sorry. I agree with Tarsea, she is the last person anyone would have expected. Maybe that is why she did it."

"What do you mean, Alex?" Starc asked.

"Perhaps she just got tired of just being someone's beautiful daughter or girlfriend. I know my friend Shirl discounts what anyone says if they start out telling her how beautiful she is." Alex got a faraway look in her eye. She was probably thinking of Shirl and worrying about how she was doing.

"Her father is a powerful man in the government and a mind control telepath. I have seen him ignore her when she said something." Solfa considered what she had said for a moment. "To be truthful, I have done the same thing when we talked at social functions. It never dawned on me that she would be so impacted by people dismissing her."

"She is always surrounded by men whenever I see her," Darden shared with the group. "This Stephano could be one of her admirers she was able to manipulate."

"The man bashed in Prime Hosp's skull," his father shared his feelings with the group. "That is certainly taking things to extremes. I am certainly glad my boys have grown into two strong minded men."

His father threw compliments out rarely. Tarsea was going to have to share what his father said with Tolfer when he got home from teaching.

"All right," Tarsea continued, "we need to discuss the next steps. Alex, did Chartail's thoughts include where she was meeting Stephano tonight?"

"Same place we had lunch. I gather it is her favorite restaurant."

Tarsea figured at this point he was going to give orders through the warrior channel. He did not want Alexandra involved in the next phase of the operation.

"I will go with Starc to the restaurant and listen to their thoughts. Once I have confirmation, Solfa, you will take over in your official capacity."

"Oh my God!" Alexandra exclaimed, temporarily stopping Tarsea from giving further orders.

"What has happened?" He looked at his soul mate and the shocked expression on her face. It was a different kind of shock than before. She almost looked excited.

"I can hear what you are saying in the warrior channel. Not only am I an intelligence officer, I am now a warrior!"

Once again, Tarsea swore under his breath.

Alex at first could not believe she was able to link into the warrior channel. Actually, it made a lot of sense. It was her intelligence that was going to bring down the remainder of the people responsible for the attempted assassination of The Prime Ruler. It also reinforced she had done the right thing in ratting out Chartail.

She could feel Tarsea's body tense next to her and he swore under his breath. He always did that when he thought he was losing control. It surprised her how well she knew this man already. Alex knew that he wanted to keep her safe and this has been just another obstacle in his pursuit to do that. She was going to have to help him manage his frustration related to her expanding role in this group.

"I am not going to go crazy and demand to go on every mission you put together." She leaned over and kissed him on his cheek. "However, I want to be involved in what you are planning and help out where I can. Don't worry, I am too much of a coward to do anything stupid."

That seemed to pacify Tarsea, at least for now. He went ahead and continued the meeting. "We will go back to talking, as well as using the warrior channel. Alex, I think you have used your telepathic abilities enough in the last couple of hours. Give that part of your brain a rest of the time being."

She nodded in agreement. There was no question she was drained. "I do have one comment on your plan so far. If I remember what you said, you can only read one mind at a time. Both Chartail and Stephano will be there, so we need two people. That means I need to be there too. I will leave when Solfa is ready to take action. Trust me, I want to be long gone when the arrests are made."

"By The Prime! Alexandra, you are not making this easy on me. Was not the incident with Raine Narmouth enough to have you be more cautious?" Tarsea complained using the mating link.

"I know, but I am right. The arrest can be postponed until I am out of the restaurant and out of harm's way, if you would like. You can work out your frustrations when we are in bed after all of this is over. Trust me, I learned my lesson related to that scum ball!"

Tarsea grinned at her, men were so easy to manipulate. It was clear she was now part of the operation. "Alexandra and I will have dinner at the restaurant. Once we get additional information regarding the plot, we will turn things over to Solfa."

Alex could see that Koel was struggling with the plan, she hoped it was not because of her.

He spoke up. "I think Chartail will be set off seeing you and Alex together in the restaurant. Since it is going to come out that Solfa and Alex are cousins, they should be the ones dining in the restaurant. We can start chatting about their relationship in the communal channels. You and Starc can be in the bar area. Just before Solfa is about to arrest them, he can get Alex out of there and bring her here."

Alex liked Koel's plan. It got her involved, but also gave her an escape route. There was a lot more to this man than the ridiculous comments he made on a regular basis.

Solfa looked at Koel and smiled. "Your plan is sound. Chartail will be distracted if the two of them are together. The plan also gets me close to the action, as well as safeguarding my cousin. Koel, Tarsea was right about your tactical abilities. I am impressed. We need to talk when this is all over."

She looked at Alex with that direct stare of hers. If Solfa wasn't her cousin, she would have been unsettled by that look. "When we are out on the town together, Alexia, I need you to stand out. No one should even get an inkling that you are part of my network."

Solfa got up and grabbed a package behind the couch. "Your aunt and my mom went shopping today and bought you this." She gave the package to Alex. "It is one of many presents you will be getting to celebrate your coming home and missed birthdays. The outfit is also appropriate for the second dinner seating. I have a feeling that Chartail and Stephano's meeting will be around that time."

Alex opened the package and pulled out a lovely tunic and leggings. The tunic was somewhat transparent, in shades of blue and white. It had pearl inlays located in strategic locations. It was absolutely breathtaking. The leggings were sheer, a beautiful aqua color. She had never worn anything so daring before.

"They purchased a number of plain tunics, as well as outfits you can go out with Tarsea and make a real impression. Men around the province will envy him." Solfa sat back on the couch next to Starc. "This one will be perfect for tonight. Evening dress is more elaborate and varied compared to what we generally wear during the day."

Alex concentrated and pushed a thank you through the familial channel to her aunt and Solfa's mother. She had never had such a gorgeous outfit before and could not wait to try it on. There was no reason in the past to have beautiful outfits, since she had never gone anywhere. She was just a little worried that she would feel a little self-conscious in the transparent tunic.

Now that Solfa had given the gift to Alex, she was all business again. "Back to the subject at hand. Tarsea, I have already cleared you joining my team with Jeryl Jarlyn. When I make the arrest, I want you to come with us. I would like to leverage you during the interview with both subjects. I know it will be difficult because it is Chartail, but it is necessary."

"I was half expecting the request. The interrogation will go much better when you know what they are thinking. We can leverage the warrior link to communicate." She could see that Tarsea was still considering this phase of the plan. "Who will be the mind control telepath in the interview?"

Solfa considered Tarsea's question. "There are a number we have used in the past. I am just not sure who I can trust at this point."

Koel sat up straighter and asked, "Have you ever leveraged my sister Tarah in the past?"

"Yes," replied Solfa, "I have. She is very good. I hate to ask, but can we trust her?"

Koel never seemed to take anyone challenging his recommendations concerning his sister personally. "She came over and interviewed both Tarsea and Alex to make sure a mind control telepath could not influence them. Tarah can be trusted."

Solfa seemed satisfied with Koel's answer. "We have our team and our plan. I will have intelligence officers nearby for the arrest. Tarsea, it is your call about how you want to leverage Darden and Koel. I will have Alex double covered by my agents. I imagine you will do the same."

"You are right," Tarsea replied. "I will have extra eyes on Alex until she is safely back in this house."

There was one thing troubling Alex, especially since it was her mind reading abilities that initiated what would happen tonight.

"What is going to happen to Chartail?" Alex knew she had to ask and she had a sinking feeling she was not going to like the answer.

Everyone looked at her, not wanting to be the one to deliver the hard news. Naturally, it was Tarsea who stepped up to the plate.

"Alex, two of the palace staff were killed during the attempt. Both of us were put in harm's way because of Chartail's actions. It is a capital crime. She will either be put to death or sent off world to the penal colony. Due to who her father is, it will probably be the penal colony."

"What is the penal colony like? I assume it is in a parallel world." Alex was very anxious about Chartail's future. She could not help feeling partly responsible for the woman's fate. Her mind kept going back to how wonderful Chartail was at lunch today. How the woman stood up to Raine Narmouth for her.

Tarsea yet again shared the difficult information with her. "There is an uninhabited world that could sustain life that we started leveraging to move our criminals to twenty-years ago. If someone is convicted of a crime that does not result in their execution, they are sent to that world for the rest of their lives. Because of the severity of the sentencing, we have very little crime here." Alex was horrified with what Tarsea just said.

"Any crime is a life sentence!" Alex said. "Is that not kind of harsh?" She still could not believe what she just heard.

"The logistics of moving from world to world is complicated. There are no guards or administrators in the penal colony world. Once the crystal telepath opens the gate, only the criminal enters the portal. It would be too complicated to manage sentences and then bring only those that had completed their term back through the gate." Alex tried to wrap her mind around what Darden said.

"I thought you said you had to enter the portal to navigate. How do you know you are sending them to this penal colony world?" Alex thought she had understood how portals worked, obviously not.

"You really listened to my explanation earlier," Darden said. "I am impressed. We partially enter the open portal and set the navigation. Once we have a stable event horizon, we step out and send the prisoners through. As long as the event horizon on the receiving side is not breached, I can exit back in the Troyk Universe with no issues."

"Can't we save her and send her through the portal to another world? You do it all the time." Alex could feel herself starting to panic. She could not imagine Chartail surrounded by rapists and murderers with no protection.

"Alex," Tarsea explained, "we help people who try to change things in a peaceful manner. Generally, they are low profile individuals who are not on anyone's immediate radar. Chartail was involved in an assassination attempt. Two innocent men are dead because of her."

For the second time this afternoon, Tarsea's father spoke up. "Alex, you are not to feel guilty that your gift helped track down Chartail before she was able to devise and execute another plan. Who knows how many people could be killed in her next attempt. The girl had everything handed to her, but still took the path she did. She is not worth one tear. Do you hear me?"

Alex got up and went to the man who was becoming the father she never had. She wrapped her arms around him and gave him a huge hug and a kiss on the cheek. A father's love is something she never had. The past several days with Zane, she realized how much she truly missed growing up without one. She wondered if her father had an extended family in this universe like her mother did.

Solfa came to her and took her hand. "Mom and Norri just got back and are loaded down with packages. Let us go and see what they bought you."

Alex followed her cousin. She would spend the afternoon opening presents and then getting ready to go out to dinner. It was the calm before the storm. She prayed everything went well tonight.

She put on her happy face and followed her cousin to relieve her aunt and cousin of the mountain of packages they hauled into the house. Her thoughts kept going back to tonight's operation. She could not help but to think about everything that could go wrong. What did she get herself into?

Chapter 24

~

Alex followed her cousin as they were being seated in the same restaurant where she had lunch, Chartail's favorite restaurant. The day had not turned out as she expected, when she walked these same steps earlier. Now that they were here, she started to think of all the things she came up with this afternoon that could go wrong. She had to remind herself this was her idea.

Rather than paying attention to the tables and how they were set, she looked at the people who occupied them. There were a number of men looking directly at Alex. She noted how their eyes traveled up and down her body. Their scrutiny of her made Alex uncomfortable. She wasn't used to this type of attention.

There was no question, the outfit her aunt and cousin selected for her was stunning. It hugged her body, caressing every single curve. The sheer material left very little to the imagination. You could see most of her breasts through the material. The pearl inlays covered her nipples. When Tarsea saw her earlier, he demanded Alex change clothes. Solfa managed to cool him down. Tonight was about the mission.

She had never worn so much makeup in her life. It almost felt as if she was wearing a disguise. Her eyes were rimmed with dark navy liner that brought out the green of her irises. Norri did an excellent job applying blush, contouring the angles of her face. Even her hair was dressed, with a thick pearl headband. Tonight was about standing out, not blending in.

They were seated at a table next to where she had lunch with Chartail. The table gave them an excellent vantage point of the bar, expecting Chartail and Stephano would start their evening there.

Two pink drinks were placed in front of them. Alex gave her aunt a questioning look.

"I ordered as we were making our way here. From what I have been able to determine so far, you will like the jerylberry cocktail." Solfa said this out loud, rather than using either the familial or warrior channel.

"The Prime Ruler has a drink named after him?" Alex asked her cousin through the familial link. She did not want to clutter the warrior pathway with non-mission chatter.

"No, the berry was named long before he was born. It is a popular fruit and a popular first name." Solfa took a sip from her drink. Alex noticed Solfa closed her eyes in appreciation of the cocktail's flavor. Her cousin did not appear nervous about tonight's operation.

Alex looked around the restaurant. On the far side of the bar, she could see both Tarsea and Starc. They were conversing with a number of other men. Unlike women, men's evening attire was the same as they wore during the day. There was nothing suspicious in how they were behaving. It appeared they were two men hanging with their friends after work.

"Here she comes," Starc communicated through the warrior channel. Alex glanced to the entrance and saw Chartail. She was stunning in white and gold. For once she was wearing a tunic and leggings. The tunic was similar to what Alex was wearing. What made her stand out from other women in the restaurant were the high heeled gold sandals she wore. Alex doubted that most men in the restaurant were looking at her feet.

She walked toward the bar, her gaze not drifting from her destination. Alex had been concerned that Chartail would spot her and come over for a short chat. What could she say to the woman she had condemned to life in a penal colony?

Chartail went up to a nondescript brown haired man who was at the bar and sat next to him. His appearance was probably why she chose him. Like Alex, the man blended into his surroundings.

They had decided earlier that she would concentrate on Chartail's thoughts and Tarsea would concentrate on Stephano's. Kohl had commented that Tarsea did not want her playing in another man's brain. One of these days Kohl was going to get a black-eye from one of his friends.

Alex took a sip from her drink and concentrated on the blonde target at the bar. It made it easier to think of her that way, rather than the woman she had lunch with this afternoon. The same woman who stood up to Raine Narmouth for her. She was getting all sorts of static, but knew she needed to work her way through it. She needed to be patient and concentrate.

"I am not getting anything yet from Stephano. One of the men we are drinking with confirmed that we are focusing on the correct man." Tarsea gave a status report through the warrior link.

"Are you all right, Alex?" Tarsea used the soul mate link to see how she was. That was really sweet of him, but she needed to concentrate.

"I'm fine. I need my entire focus on Chartail to pick up her thoughts. Sorry, I need to cut you off." She would make it up to him tonight when they were alone in their room.

Alex went back to concentrating on her subject. There was still too much static. She took another sip of her drink, hoping it would help calm her nerves.

The static changed suddenly. Alex focused on Chartail. *"I cannot believe this loser thinks he can blackmail me. He was the one who messed up the mission and now he wants money. At least he took care of Hosp."*

"I have a confirmation the man sitting next to her killed Prime Hosp." Alex shared through the warrior link. It was her first official communication through that channel.

"Nothing yet from target number two. He keeps thinking about having sex with Chartail." Tarsea shared with the group in disgust, again leveraging the warrior pathway. For a bare second, Alex wondered if Tarsea was jealous.

The waiter came and set a dish of appetizers on the table. *"That is all I ordered. I figured you would not be too hungry, considering. We also needed to order something so we would not draw attention to ourselves."* Solfa shared with her, as she bit into one of the items served.

"And this dress does not draw attention to us?" Alex asked sarcastically through the familial link. Solfa's dress was more conservative. Alex wondered what her cousin wore when she really went out for the evening.

Her cousin smiled. *"We will give them ten more minutes before I shut down the first phase of this operation. If nothing happens in the meantime, Starc come here and pick Alex up at the end of the ten minutes. Maybe the drink will relax the man's mind."*

Alex popped an appetizer in her mouth. She was not sure what it was. For the first time since coming to the Troyk Universe, she could not taste anything. Her stomach was doing somersaults.

Chartail still had her back to Alex, which she found a relief. She really hoped she could get out of here before the woman spotted her. This was going to be the longest ten minutes of her life.

The static cleared again and Alex was ready to receive another thought. *"That bastard Tarsea is at the end of the bar. Too bad I could not have leveraged him, he would not have messed things up as Stephano and Gerred did. I bet he is already two timing that sweet Alexia."*

"Chartail mentioned a Gerred. Was he one of the men who was killed during the failed attack? She also spotted Tarsea." Alex hoped they did not have a third suspect on the loose that could put her soul mate in danger. She did not share the last part of Chartail's thought.

"One of the men killed during the attack was Gerred Sloan." Solfa shared the information with the group. Alex was relieved, she exhaled the breath she had been holding.

She looked up and saw that Raine Narmouth was being seated with some woman. Alex was not sure if he saw her. She did not want to upset the mission alerting everyone to his presence.

"Got it! Stephano just thought about plotting with Chartail. He is now blackmailing her. Starc, head over to Alex and get her the hell out of here. Phase one is now officially over. Phase two will commence when Alex has been removed from the premises. Solfa is now on point. Koel, keep your position outside the restaurant, even after Alex and Starc leave." Alex could almost hear the relief in her soul mate's voice.

She could see Starc was making his way to their table, when all hell broke loose.

"Stefano for some reason has left his stool and it appears he plans to leave." Tarsea let the group know. *"He may have recognized one of Solfa's men."*

The intelligence officers at the bar went to stop Stefano from leaving and he drew a weapon. There was a scream and the communal channel was full of chatter about someone having a gun. People in the bar and the restaurant started to leave in a panic.

People in the bar were pushing and shoving to get out. Alex could not see Starc with all the confusion and bodies appearing to be bouncing off each other.

"Alex get out of here!" Solfa cried. *"Two of my men will be nearby. Starc will no doubt connect with you outside the restaurant."* With those words her cousin went to join the chaos in the bar. Alex watched her dodge people leaving the restaurant.

She had taken a couple of steps when she felt someone grab her arm. She looked up, expecting to see Starc, only to see Raine Narmouth. He was dragging her in the direction of the restaurant's exit. It was the direction she wanted to go. Besides, if she tried to fight him, she may get trampled by the people behind her trying to leave the premises. Once outside, she would free herself of his presence. The crowd pushed her forward and Raine still had a vice like grip on her arm. His date was nowhere in sight.

They were just short of the restaurant's exit when Raine's arms coiled around her. She could feel them falling, with Raine controlling the fall in order that she would take the brunt of the impact. Alex came down hard on the floor, her head hitting the tile. The wind was knocked out of her and Raine's body pinned her to the ground.

Raine took her head in his hands. "Sorry, baby," he whispered in her ear, as he proceeded to pound her skull onto the floor several times. "We cannot have you calling for help through the communal pathways. It is finally time for the two of us to spend some time together."

Raine stood, taking Alex with him. She was somewhat disoriented and could not hear any static in her head. He stuffed a cloth napkin in her mouth and then lifted her into his arms. Smothering her against his chest, as he followed the crowd out of the restaurant. Her muffled cries were drowned out by the noise of people shouting around her. Raine had also managed to pin her arms together with one of his large hands.

Bodies still bumped into Raine as he continued to carry her. She could sense they were still surrounded by people. She tried the various pathways she had leveraged in the past with no success. Even the soul mate pathway appeared to be impacted by the blows Raine inflicted to her head. The confusion in the restaurant must have distracted the intelligence officers that were supposed to be protecting her. She could only hope that Koel or Darden had spotted them and were on their way to rescue her.

It felt like fewer people were scrambling against them and she started to feel foliage brushing up against her body. They must have arrived at the walking trails. If he took her on one of the paths, it would be harder for any of the team to find them.

As she continued to struggle, Raine held her face closer to his chest. It had reached a point she could no longer breathe. Her struggles turned into a life or death fight. She frantically twisted her body in an attempt to loosen his grip on her face in order to grab a breath.

Alex could feel her strength wane, her last thoughts were of Tarsea. *"I love you, Tarsea,"* she helplessly pushed into the soul mate channel. She would die without ever saying those words to him, knowing he would not be able to hear her through the soul mate link.

She felt Raine release his hold on her head as he placed her on a bed of leaves and twigs. He pulled the napkin out of her mouth. Alex gasped, filling her lungs with much needed oxygen. Raine's full weight pressing against her body, adversely impacting her ability to regulate her breathing. Both her arms were pinned underneath her, she could not pull them free. With one hand, Raine grabbed at her clothing. His other hand was once again covering her mouth, preventing her from screaming.

Raine was pulling at her leggings, as Alex tried one more desperate attempt at communicating through the soul mate channel. *"Tarsea, please help me. Raine is going to rape me if you don't get here in time."* She had to have faith the soul mate pathway was everything Tarsea said it was. Although Raine did a number on her head, the soul mate pathway would be the first channel to repair itself.

She continued to fight as best she could, but she knew she was fighting a losing battle. Her strength had been negatively impacted by her temporary loss of air. Raine's hand was caressing her upper thigh. He kept muttering in her ear words she could not comprehend.

"Alex, where are you?" She heard Tarsea's voice in her head. Thank God, the pathway repaired itself. He had been in the bar area of the restaurant when the chaos began, if he was still there, he may not be able to get to her in time.

"I am somewhere off one of the walking paths. Raine dragged me back here, but I could not see where he took me." After communicating with Tarsea, Alex had her second wind to intensify her struggles against Raine. She just needed to buy some time.

"Alexia, please, stop struggling," Raine pleaded. "I love you. We were meant to be together. Let me touch and taste you, nothing more. Our first time together will be on satin sheets, I promise." His mouth replaced his hand over her mouth.

Alex deepened his kiss, hoping he would think she was now interested and slow down the urgency of his attack. He must have been surprised by her response, because he pulled back and lifted his head to look at her.

"I know you are my soul mate, Alexia. If we spend some more time together, I know the telepathic channel will open between the two of us." Raine proceeded to kiss her again. Alex did her best not to show her revulsion to his kiss and his touch. His other hand continued to caress her thigh, but did not breach her panties.

Suddenly she felt the pressure on her body lessen, as Raine was lifted off her. In the dim light, she saw Tarsea and Starc dragging Raine away.

"Alex, take my hand. I will help you up," Tolfer said. He was once again at her side after being attacked by Raine. She grabbed his arm and slowly stood up. It was not surprising she was a little light headed.

Not far away, she heard Tarsea giving orders. "Koel and Starc, guard the pathways. I do not want to be interrupted."

"What is going on?" Alex inquired. She looked and saw Tarsea and Raine squaring off. "Are you insane? Turn him over to the authorities, let him rot on the penal colony world." She could not believe her eyes.

She started to make her way over to the two men, when Tolfer held her back. "You know we cannot do that, Alex. There would be inquiries and questions asked." Damn, he was right. However, there had to be a better idea than Tarsea fighting the man one on one. Raine Narmouth was a snake and she did not trust him to fight fair.

Alex watched as Raine took a swing at Tarsea. He dodged the attack and initiated a jab to Raine's left side. Unlike Tarsea, Raine was not fast enough to avoid the blow. Unfortunately, Tarsea had come in close to his opponent to make contact and was immediately hit in the jaw with a right hook. He let out a moan as Raine made contact.

Instinct took over, Alex stepped in to aid Tarsea. Tolfer held her back yet again. She could not understand how the other men would let Tarsea fight him alone. They should have ganged up on Raine and made mincemeat of his face and body.

As she was struggling against Tolfer's hold, Raine yet again connected with Tarsea's face. Where did that bastard learn to fight? Tarsea recovered quickly, connecting with Raine's midsection. Both men pulled back, no doubt determining their next strategic move. She could see Tarsea's face was beginning to bruise and blood was running from his nose.

She needed to stop this somehow. *"Solfa, you need to come to the Gathering Place walking paths. Tarsea and Raine are fighting. You need to stop this and arrest the bastard who tried to rape me."* Alex used the warrior link, she did not want to alarm her aunt or Solfa's mother.

Her soul mate was built like a bull, compared to Raine's height and his reach. Tarsea charged Raine with his mass, forcefully slamming Raine into a trunk of a tree. Alex hoped that would momentarily disorient Raine, giving Tarsea additional time to finish off the job. Tarsea took the advantage and punch the bastard in the face.

Alex's sigh of relief was short lived when she saw Raine reach behind him and pull out some kind of object. Through the warrior channel she could hear Tolfer yell, *"Knife, look out, Tarsea!"*

What happened next almost appeared to occur in slow motion. Alex watched helplessly as Raine drove the knife into Tarsea. "No!" she yelled, as Tolfer released her and she made her way to her soul mate. She watched in horror as Tarsea fell where he stood.

Raine had backed away from Tarsea, as Alex fell to her knees next to her love. The knife was embedded in his side. She was never good at anatomy and was not sure what major organs may have been impacted by the knife. Alex sat helplessly, not knowing what to do, other than comfort her soul mate.

"It is going to be all right, baby," Tarsea told her just before he passed out.

"Oh God, what do I do?" Alex asked no one in particular. Tolfer was kneeling next to her, seeing to his brother's injuries to the best of his ability. He removed his tunic and carefully wrapped it around the protruding knife, trying to control the bleeding.

From the corner of her eye, she saw Raine turn and run, only to come in direct contact with Starc. The men were going to come to blows, just as Solfa arrived.

"Arrest this man for assault," Solfa ordered the two men that followed her.

"I was only protecting what is mine," Raine replied. "Childers attacked me, I was defending myself. You did not hear anything in the communal pathway from Alexia asking for help. She was with me willingly. It is my word against his. I am a Crystal Telepath Guard Captain, I demand respect!"

"My cousin does not belong to you. No man would treat the woman he loves the way you treated her tonight." For the first time, Alex looked down and was horrified at how exposed her body was. Her sheer tunic was ripped in a number of places and there was little covering the front of her chest. Frankly, she was too concerned about Tarsea to care.

"There is nothing your father or your mind control telepathic brother can do for you now," Starc added to the conversation.

"Get him out of my sight," Solfa ordered her subordinates. She knelt next to Alex and examined Tarsea.

As they forcefully led Raine Narmouth away, Alex could hear his pleas for her to stand up for him. The man was delusional. Everything he shouted fell on deaf ears, all white noise. Her world had collapsed to just the man bleeding in front of her. She was thankful Koel was following the men that took Raine away. He would assure Narmouth did not escape on the way to where ever they were going to hold him.

Solfa made short work of her examination of Tarsea. "I need a med-tech immediately," she shouted to one of her officers. "We have technology you could not fathom for injuries such as these, Alexia. Our first consideration is to make sure he does not bleed out before the tech arrives. It looks like Tolfer had done a great job doing just that."

With Raine Narmouth no longer a threat, Starc came to squat on the other side of Tarsea. He proceeded to take off his tunic and handed it to her. "Put this on, Alex," Starc said. "We do not want Tarsea to wake and have to kill us all for basking on your beauty." She smiled as she slipped on his tunic.

"Thank you, Starc," Alex replied. "My Tarsea would do exactly that." If Tarsea would just be all right, she would never complain about his possessiveness again. She prayed, for the first time in years, for her soul mate's life.

A man all in white arrived and knelt next to Starc. "Everyone needs to back away from the patient. I need room to examine and work on him." Alex sighed with relief. She got to her feet and moved to stand behind the man, as he started working on her soul mate.

The med-tech pulled out what looked like a tablet and directed it toward the wound. The display showed what appeared to be a live action x-ray. Although she was no doctor, it did not appear that any of the organs were cut by the knife. She waited for the med-tech to provide some kind of prognosis. He pulled out a bag of fluid and stuck the needle attached to the bag into his arm. Alex did not know what was in the fluid, but she took it as a good sign.

"I am going to pull out the knife now. Can you gentlemen hold him down, just in case he awakens while I am removing the blade? We do not want him twisting and doing additional damage." Tolfer and Starc did as the med-tech requested, while he pulled out the knife in one swift motion. "Hold the tunic against the wound."

The med-tech reached for what looked like a sonic screwdriver from an episode of 'Dr. Who.' The tool started to glow as he pushed away Tolfer's hand holding his tunic against the wound. He placed it against the exposed area and Alex watched in wonder as the cut flesh started to close. He continued to hold it over the repaired skin. Alex assumed it was healing the internal rip that the knife caused.

After several minutes, the sonic screwdriver was put away and the med-tech gave Tarsea an injection. "What was that for?" Alex inquired.

"The medication will accelerate the production of blood by the body ten times the normal rate. A wonderful drug that was brought back from the Nightshade universe. Wounds such as these are easily healed, assuming the patient does not bleed out or an organ is damaged beyond our ability to repair. He should be coming around any time now." She had heard the words earlier, but seeing was truly believing. The med-tech started putting away his other equipment, as Tarsea started to wake, just as the tech said he would.

"Are you all right, Alex?" were Tarsea's first words. Her emotions got the best of her and she started to cry.

"Am I all right? You were the one stabbed, you stupid man. How can you endanger yourself like that? There were four of you. Why did you have to fight him alone? You should have beat the crap out of him and then sent him through the portal to some hell hole of a universe. Just like Starc recommended the other day." Words just spilled out of Alex's mouth. Her internal filters generally in place when she was in control were non-existent.

The med-tech pulled the IV out of Tarsea's arm. "Let us see if we can get you standing," he said. The three men helped Tarsea to his feet. It appeared his stability was good, as they released their hold on him. "I think my work is done here. Just take it easy the next couple of days. Drink as much fluid as possible."

Alex went up to the man and hugged him. He had saved her soul mate's life. A simple 'thank you' seemed inadequate. The man simply nodded and walked away.

"Starc, take Alexia home. Tarsea and I still have a long evening ahead of us," Solfa said.

"You cannot be serious," Alexandra cried. "He was just stabbed! Tarsea needs to go home and rest. We have had enough for one night. Between you and Tarah, you should be able to get a confession out of Chartail and Stephano. I am taking Tarsea home." Alex grabbed Tarsea's sleeve and started to pull, expecting him to leave with her.

"It is not that easy, Alex," Tarsea said. "As long as the brain is not impacted or an organ is not severely damaged, our technology enables almost immediate recovery from injuries.

Alex stared at her soul mate, dumbfounded. The events of the evening played over in her head. Just moments before she was leaning over what she thought was her mortally wounded love. She looked at the blood that covered the ground upon which they stood. "Look at that," Alex pointed to the crimson soaked ground. "You were bleeding out, Tarsea. The med-tech gave you some fluids and an injection, but that is it. You need to be in bed."

Solfa placed her hands on Alex's shoulders. "You are in the Troyk Universe now, stop thinking like someone from Ginkgo Terra. The communal channels know we arrested two suspects in the assassination attempt. Jeryl Jarlyn will expect an interrogation and confession this evening, with Tarsea involved. He is healed and ready for duty based on our standards."

"Go with Starc, I will be fine," Tarsea said. He brought Alex into his arms and kissed her forehead. He then addressed his brother, "Thank you, Tolfer. I owe you a new tunic."

Alex stared in disbelief as Tarsea and Solfa walked away. As soon as she thought she had figured out her new world, a curve ball was thrown. There was still so much to learn.

She looked at the man standing next to her. "Starc, what happened between you and Raine Narmouth?" Alex asked. His tunic almost came down to her knees, another reminder the violence that occurred tonight. Nothing would make her happier than to have Raine sentenced to the penal world. Originally, she had been horrified by the idea of such a place, but now it seemed like an appropriate place for the man.

"I really do not want to talk about it. Let us just say that you are not the first woman he attacked. You at least had the ability to fight him off." A cloud fell over Starc's face. Alex imagined he was thinking about that other woman.

"What happened to her?" Alex asked, she really wanted to know. It bothered her that Raine had a violent history against women, but she was not warned with more particulars not to date the man.

Starc stopped and looked at Alex. "Please, I do not want to talk about it."

Alex had to respect Starc's wishes, although her curiosity was piqued. For a fraction of a second she considered reading his mind. She quickly dismissed that thought. Starc was a friend. When he wanted to share what happened between them he could. Best to change topics. Might as well learn more about the workings of the Troyk world as they made their way home.

"So, Starc," Alex continued, "tell me all about what it means to be a Crystal Telepath Guard."

She listened to Starc's explanation, hoping to also pick up chatter in the warrior link. Was Tarsea really all right?

Tarsea drew in a deep breath as Starc communicated they were heading to his parents' house. He had seen the hurt and confusion in Alex's eyes as he left her behind to continue the mission. He had planted Darden and Koel close by in case the mission went badly. Tolfer was there just for Alex's protection if necessary. There was no question he had spent a good part of the operation watching Alex's surroundings. She was a different type of target wearing that damn tunic that exposed more of her than he liked. With all his precautions,

Raine was still able to get to her tonight. Had he hit her head a little harder, it was possible the soul mate channel may not have repaired itself in time for him to reach her.

He had not missed Raine Narmouth coming into the restaurant. The man appeared to be on a date, but he kept an eye on him as well. Alex had seen him, but correctly did not voice anything in the warrior channel. It was a crowded restaurant, so she would be perfectly safe. Besides, she was dining with her cousin, who, if the rumors were true, could be as lethal as any man. He also had his three men outside the restaurant as back up if Narmouth tried anything.

When Stephano made his move and pandemonium resulted, he had lost sight of Alex in the rush of people exiting the restaurant. At that point the mission was scrubbed in his mind. He tried to find Alex in the rush of people. As if the patrons of the restaurant and bar were not enough to deal with, a crowd gathered outside, curious by all the commotion within the communal pathway. He kept trying to reach Alex through the soul mate channel, but could not connect with her. Tarsea had a pretty good idea that Narmouth must have caused some kind of head injury to her, preventing her from reaching out for help.

It had only been eight minutes of silence within their link, but it was an eternity to him. He and his friends searched among the crowd and the surrounding area for her. Tarsea had even sent Darden to Narmouth's residence in case he took her directly there.

Relief flowed through Tarsea when he finally heard from Alexandra. When he found his soul mate and saw Raine on top of her, a rage he had never experienced overcame him. He was going to tear the man apart. Tarsea positioned Koel and Starc on the path so he would not be interrupted. However, he had not expected Narmouth to be as good a fighter as he was. He had finally had the fight going in his favor when the bastard pulled a knife. Tarsea had heard Tolfer's cry, but the blade was driven into his side before he could react.

The pain of the knife lodged in his side had caused him to lose consciousness, or maybe it was the loss of blood. He will always remember waking and seeing Alexandra kneeling over him. It tore him apart when he had to leave her, in order to complete the mission. During all the chaos, both Chartail and

Stephano had been apprehended and arrested. He needed to fulfill his obligation and participate in their interrogations.

The eight intelligence officers had already taken their prisoners to The Palace. They were just awaiting their arrival to start the interrogations. Tarsea would not be surprised if a decision would be made tonight regarding the fate of both Chartail and Stephano.

Unknown to most Aster Province residents, there were also holding cells in the basement of The Palace. Suspects were held there until guilt or innocence was determined. Convicted individuals were held until their sentence could be commenced. Either way, Chartail was going to sleep this evening in The Palace's basement.

Solfa was still beside him when they exited the walking path. *"We can head over to The Palace together. I have a feeling it will be a long evening."* This type of communication was safe through the communal channel. The more they could communicate in the public channels, the better. People would start to wonder why they were not more actively engaged in communal discussions. Generally, when he communicated in the warrior channel, he was sharing some inane piece of news in a communal pathway for appearances.

As they walked to the Aster Province Palace, Tarsea listened to the chatter within the different communal pathways. They were saturated with conversations about the arrests and what happened at the restaurant. He did not bother giving Alexandra an update. She was probably listening to all the activity in the communal channels, while drinking her herbal mixture. He also knew that Tolfer was there helping her manage the unusually high volume of activity within the pathways. If her brain still had not picked up the communal pathways, he was sure his parents and Tolfer were informing her of everything being communicated.

It took little time before they came upon The Palace and headed in. The interviews would be conducted in two of the conference rooms on the third floor. His interview yesterday was on the same floor.

"The interviews will be done orally, unless one or both of the suspects goes into a communal pathway. I will conduct the interview, Tarah will leverage mind control, and you will see if you can read their minds. If you get anything, communicate through the warrior pathway. We will start with Chartail. Any questions?" Solfa was efficient, Tarsea could say that for her.

169

"I am ready," was all Tarsea had to say. He was going to be a party to sending a lovely woman to hell. She had started the chain of events, but he could not help but feel some guilt there. If their relationship had more substance, maybe she would have confided in him about her feelings related to mind control. He would have gotten her involved in his organization in some capacity.

Tarah Mardroft walked toward them, and Solfa opened the door to the conference room where Chartail was held.

Chartail was alone, with three chairs set up directly in front of her. Her eye makeup was smeared from crying. The tunic she wore had a small rip on the shoulder. Seeing Chartail this way, he could not help but think about how messed up his little pixie looked after her ordeal with Narmouth this evening. After everything she had been through, Alexandra had been fierce in her determination to have him accompany her home and rest.

The prisoner looked up as they entered. "What happened to you?" she asked Tarsea. Although the med-tech healed his knife wound, his face was still bruised from the fight with the bastard.

"Narmouth attacked Alexia again," Tarsea answered her.

He could not help but see the look of concern for his soul mate cross Chartail's face. "Is she all right?"

"She was pretty messed up, but she will be fine."

"Did you kill him?" Chartail asked.

"No, he was arrested." Tarsea replied. He wondered if he will ultimately have to kill him. Narmouth seemed to be insanely infatuated with Alexandra.

"You should have killed him." Chartail turned her attention to Solfa and said, "Let us get on with this. It is late and I want to go home."

Solfa got the interrogation going. "Chartail Anholm, you are accused of being part of the conspiracy to assassinate our Prime Ruler. I will be conducting your interrogation. Tarah Mardroft will be present as the interview's mind control telepath. She will be able to tell if you are lying to us. Tarsea Childers is present as one of my intelligence officers."

"You son of a bitch!" Chartail yelled, glaring at Tarsea. "You were spying on me the whole time you were sharing my bed."

Tarsea was thankful she was restrained. Otherwise, she would have been all over him trying to scratch out his eyes. He had never seen this side of her.

Solfa tried to calm Chartail. "Chartail, control yourself. You are not doing yourself any favors. We are talking about possibly taking your life if you are found guilty of these charges."

Chartail paled at those words and quieted. Solfa continued the interview. "We will speak orally for your own protection, but you are free to be interrogated within one of the communal channels. The choice is yours."

"Orally is fine. I did not do anything related to the attempt on Jarlyn's life. He is one of my father's best friends and a colleague. I have known him my whole life." Chartail started crying and looked up at her accusers with tears rolling down her cheeks.

"Two of the three statements she made are true. Her father is a friend of Jarlyn's and she has known him her whole life. Miss Adholm, I am a mind control telepath. I can tell when someone is lying. You lied when you said you did not do anything related to the attempt on Jarlyn's life."

Tarsea could see Chartail's face change before his eyes. Gone was the shattered innocent woman. In her place was an angry and bitter one. "All you mind control telepathic shit heads are the same. You are so above everyone else, like my father and our Prime Ruler. I see the disappointment in my father's eyes every day. I am defective because I cannot manipulate the mind of others in his opinion. What they do is wrong and deplorable. People should be able to make their own decisions about what government they want to live under. Jeryl Jarlyn deserved to die, as well as any other mind control telepathic freaks who use their gift in a sorted way."

"I am not needed here anymore," Tarsea communicated to Solfa. Chartail had incriminated herself beyond repair. She could have shared half-truths and been absolved. His ability to read thoughts could not be shared with Prime Ruler Jarlyn.

"I am sorry, Chartail. If I had been a better boyfriend, maybe this could have been prevented." Tarsea got up to leave.

Naturally, Chartail had to have the last word. "Are you serious? You were great in bed, but you are a coward. I saw how you cozied up to them. How you became rich by their manipulation of the masses."

He turned and walked out of the room. Everything she said was true. His cover had been so convincing that the woman he had a relationship with for seven months, did not have a clue who he really was. As he continued on his way, he transmitted to Solfa through the warrior's link. *"Please do not have Darden take Chartail to the portal after her sentencing."*

He heard someone running behind him and stopped. Turning, he saw Tarah Mardroft coming toward him. "Tarsea, I heard you say that you were not needed here anymore. It felt weird. The words came through a channel I had never used before. Can you explain that?"

Tarsea did not have the mental fortitude to explain the warrior link to Tarah tonight. He put his hand on her shoulder as a confirming welcome. "Ask your brother when you are alone with him." He spoke the words out loud, he had enough of telepathic communication tonight.

He turned and left The Palace. All he wanted to do was go home and see Alexandra. Chartail's fate would be all over the communal channels when a decision was made. Tonight he just wanted to be buried in Alex, body and soul.

Chapter 25

~

Tarsea had never been happier to be home in his life. All he wanted to do was hold his soul mate in his arms. There was an intimacy which he needed more than taking his next breath.

Alexandra was in the common room with his parents. She was wearing a cushy robe that engulfed her whole body. He could not help but smile. His little pixie looked that much smaller in the enormous robe. She was adorable. More important, she cleansed his soul. Just seeing her revived him to some extent.

She got up when he walked into the room. Concern was written on her face, as she came into his arms. "How are you? Has a verdict regarding Chartail's fate been handed down?" He thought it odd that she had just met his former girl-friend, but her thoughts immediately went to the ill-fated woman.

He kissed her head and held her tight before he addressed her questions. "I am fine. Tarah caught her in a lie immediately. I did not have to scan her mind for her thoughts. As soon as it was clear that I was not needed, I left. She gave up herself and Stephano. The communal pathways will let us know as soon as Jarlyn has made a decision about their fates."

Tarsea hugged both his parents. He knew that Alex had shared everything that had happened this evening with them. It was important his parents could see he was fine. "I love you both. There is no more that can be done tonight. I am taking Alex to our room."

His parents wished them a good night and he walked with his soul mate to their bedroom. They had a unique understanding how much Alex and he needed each other after the events of the day.

When they reached their room, Alex sat on the bed as he took off his tunic, leggings, and shoes. Although the med-tech healed his wound, he knew he was black and blue. Surface wounds were never deemed critical enough to heal.

'Baby, I just want to hold you and talk if that is all right. "He walked to his side of the bed and laid down. Tarsea could not remember the last time he was so weary. He needed the girl with the bright green eyes to restore him.

Alex joined him, snuggling next to him. For some reason, she did not remove what she had been wearing. "Why are you still wearing the robe? Would you not be more comfortable without it?" Although he had not planned to make love tonight because of her ordeal, he did want to hold her nude body.

"Later, I will take it off, later." She took her hands and started to massage his temples. It felt great. "Tell me what happened at The Palace."

Tarsea closed his eyes and just held her for a moment longer before he began. "She held our beliefs and I did not even know it. I had never seen that side of Chartail before. There was so much hatred seething from her."

Alex appeared to be taking in what he told her and mulling it over in her mind. "How well do we know anyone, unless they really let us in? Most people just know the person we present to the world. Chartail did not have a positive outlet to let her anger go. She must not have had a true friend."

"Baby, I question if our ability to read minds is as offensive as mind control. We would be able to see what people do not want to present to anyone." He had to confess these doubts to his soul mate.

Alex shoved his shoulder. "We don't influence what people are thinking or what actions they are going to take. Yes, it is an invasion of privacy, but it is not in the same league with the manipulation mind control telepathic individuals practice.

"We are fighting a war and we have to leverage every weapon we have at our disposal. Besides, there is also a lot of bad in our world. If I had read Raine's mind and saw what he was really like, I certainly would not have gone out with him!"

She whacked him again, obviously Alex was not done yet challenging what Tarsea confided in her. "There is no question what we do can be abused, so we will have to have these discussions on a regular basis to make sure we are not going too far. Chartail's actions ended up with two innocent men dying. If the people responsible for the plot were not found soon, Darden said they were going to put guards around the portal. That would adversely impact you rescuing others. Not to mention getting Shirl here. I like Chartail, I will admit that. She stood up to Narmouth and for that I am grateful. However, I am not going to sacrifice Shirl for someone who was responsible for the death of two men."

Tarsea imagined it would take some time before the guilt associated with Chartail was going to diminish. It felt good talking to Alexandra in this manner. She was right, they needed to have these talks on a regular basis. They had a powerful gift to read people's minds. A gift that could be manipulated to support the wrong causes. Together, as soul mates, they needed to constantly gauge if they were doing the right things.

"I do have a confession to make though," Alex said. "This evening I was tempted for an instant to read Starc's mind in order to discover what caused the bad blood between him and Narmouth. I rejected the idea almost as quickly as I considered it. It just represents how seductive this power is and how we have to manage our abilities."

He imagined it took a great deal of courage for her to confess what she had considered doing to Starc. Tarsea had been struggling with leveraging mind control to stop Narmouth, although he was not ready to tell her that. He did feel he needed to share the thoughts he had as of late regarding how frustrated he had been related to the lack of progress they were making.

"Since we are making confessions," Tarsea added, "I have one to make as well. In my desire for change to happen faster, I have questioned our decision to take the peaceful route. When we found out about Chartail, a part of me wondered what I would have done if she had approached me."

"You are a good man, Tarsea. It's easy to second guess yourself. Violence is just not who you are. Taking that action would possibly get you there faster, but you would not be able to live with yourself afterwards. Thinking about something is very different than acting on it."

Her words warmed his soul, he loved this woman. He rolled over, lying on top of his little pixie in the ridiculous robe. His mouth covered hers in a kiss he had been wanting to give her all evening. She looked incredible tonight. He deepened the kiss as this erection grew harder.

Alex started pounding on his chest. "Let me up!"

Tarsea rolled off her, guilt consuming him. After what she had been through tonight, how could he have laid on top of her like that?

She stood next to the bed. All of a sudden she got a mischievous look on her face. "Solfa went shopping this afternoon, even with everything else going on. She got me my first naughty lingerie. I had planned to surprise you tonight and wear it. There is no way I am going to let what happened with Raine Narmouth mess up our evening." With those words she took off the robe she had been wearing.

Tarsea basked his eyes on what Alexandra was wearing. It was a sheer black teddy that was slit at the bottom, showing off her perfect belly button. Through the thin material he could see her nipples grow harder as his eyes drank in the sight of her. She wore sheer black panties that appeared to have an open crotch. Her body was bruised, but her eyes sent out an invitation he was not about to decline.

"Remind me to find out where Solfa bought that lingerie. I will make sure we have a drawer free in the dresser for more naughty items. We will get a pair in every color." He maneuvered to where she stood and took her into his arms.

Tarsea pulled Alex onto the bed and rolled on top of her. He decided he needed to further examine the outfit his soul mate had on. His mouth went over her left breast and started to suck on the nipple through the sheer material. It continued to grow harder under his care. He could hear little mews coming from her throat. With his fingers, he explored to verify the panties were indeed crotchless. To his utter delight, they were. He took one finger and entered through her feminine folds. Playing with her clit as he started working on the other breast.

"Is this all right, baby?" Tarsea asked. He knew he was touching her intimately and wanted to make sure he had not gone too far.

"Yes!" Alex said as she was moving under him. He took a second finger and entered her. His fingers increased their pace and she fractured as she came. Her juices covered his fingers as he removed them from her body. She was ready for all of him.

For the first time since they started making love, he entered her slowly. One excruciating inch at a time. She always took things slowly when she was in control, he wanted to show her he could show some self-discipline as well.

He had gone as far as he could when Alex brought her legs around his waist, which drove him in deeper. Tarsea increased the rate of his thrusts and Alex met his pace. They climaxed at the same time. He captured her scream with his mouth, in a searing kiss.

Spent, Tarsea collapsed on Alex, too exhausted to move. She muttered something, which he did not understand. The words finally ended up coming through the soul mate channel, *"I think I may be falling in love with you, Tarsea. It's only been six days and you are a man whore and all, but I'm pretty sure I'm a goner."*

He came down beside her, and gathered her in his arms. *"I am a reformed man-whore, which I plan to prove to you. I feel things for you I have never felt for another woman. I know what you said about the soul mate legends impacting my feelings, but I really do love you. My life changed when you came through that portal. I knew it the minute I saw you. It was reinforced when I opened my eyes this evening and you were there."*

"It was dumb luck that I came through. There were so many things that could have transpired preventing me from ever coming over to you."

"We were worlds apart, baby. Destiny would have found a way to bring us together." Tarsea could not imagine what life would have been like had his little pixie with her large boots had not come through the portal.

He continued to hold Alexandra as she drifted to sleep. She knew so little of his world. They had sheltered her regarding what a death sentence really meant. The other worlds that were out there and the unholy alliances the Troyk had with many of those worlds. He only hoped she would look at him with the same light in her eyes when she started learning about these secrets.

Chapter 26

~

Alex slowly opened her eyes. Tarsea was still sleeping next to her. She figured with him still in bed, it had to be early. The sun must have just started rising. Tinted violet light crept into the room through the window.

She listened to the sounds of the morning. Birds chirped, while she heard a squirrel noisily run up the tree branch outside the window. It was even too early to hear Leenea or Tolfer working in the kitchen. Her head was on Tarsea's chest. She could hear his heartbeat and his even breathing. This is how she wanted to wake up every morning.

Yawning, she decided to go back to sleep, when there was a commotion in the communal pathway. Tarsea woke up with a start.

They looked at each other as they listened to what was being communicated. Tarsea looked at her in utter disbelief, when they learned that Chartail and her accomplice were both sentenced to death for their part in the assassination attempt on the Prime Ruler.

"How could he come to that verdict? She is the daughter of his closest political associate?" Alex was stunned. All this time she thought Chartail would be sent to the penal colony, not executed. She was hit with a wave of nausea.

"There were witnesses present when she was brought before Jeryl Jarlyn. He was expecting her to beg for mercy. She did nothing of the sort. Chartail denounced mind control and Jarlyn. It sounded like she gave him no choice." Alex could see the guilt in Tarsea's eyes as he said those words.

Tarsea was able to navigate the communal channel far better than she could. She was grateful he was sharing what he was hearing. When Tolfer had the time, she needed to continue her studies in better managing the pathways.

"Prime Anholm never went to the palace to be with or speak on behalf of his daughter," Tarsea shared with her. He was still listening to what was coming across and vocalizing what he was hearing.

"My God, she was all alone," Alex could not fathom such a thing. She knew if anything happened to her, Shirl and Candy would be right beside her. Now she had Tarsea, their families and friends as well. She had evidence of that due to the run-ins with Raine.

She had not expected to shed any more tears for Chartail. With the news this morning, a whole new set of tears started rolling down her cheeks.

Tarsea held her close and let her shed the tears for a girl he could not shed them for. Alex knew that from the haunted look in his eyes last night, he wished he could cry for the loss of Chartail.

After a while the tears ceased, but Tarsea did not release her. She still found comfort being in his arms.

She got up the courage and finally asked the question burning in her mind. "How will she be executed?" Alex thought of all the ways they ended lives in her old world. She had never believed in capital punishment.

Some time had passed and Tarsea still had not answered her question. "Tarsea?"

He pulled away and looked her in the eye. She saw the desperation in his eyes. "Please, do not ask me. Maybe one day I can tell you, but not today."

Her question was tearing him apart and that was the last thing she wanted. It did not really matter how they killed Chartail, the result was the same. That beautiful girl would never find the soul mate that Alex was fortunate enough to have found.

"That is all right. I really do not want to know. It is best I remember her the way she was at lunch yesterday." Alex did not think she could ever be able to see a bright color and not think of Chartail's tragic life.

One lesson to learn from the events of yesterday was to value what you had. Dwelling on what you did not have was counterproductive. She had the best man in the world right next to her. What else could she possibly want?

That question was answered quickly. Shirl, Candy, and Jo Jo. They belonged in this world. They belonged with her.

"When is Darden entering the portal to bring Shirl to the Troyk Universe?" Alex ached for her best friend. She had so much to say to her about what had happened the last several days.

She wondered what Shirl and Candy would think about the new Alex. They would have applauded if they had seen her in last night's outfit. The Troyk Universe had changed her. There were times since she came through the portal, she did not recognize herself.

"He is scheduled to go through the portal the day after tomorrow. I want to go with him and meet Benko Jarlyn. It is time we go on the offensive and start making plans." She knew Tarsea was playing 'what if' games in his head. Had they gotten Benko Jarlyn here earlier and in power, Chartail would not be facing death.

"Would it be easier if I came with the two of you? Shirl may be more willing to come along if I was with you."

Tarsea got a big smile on his face. "You are asking, rather than demanding?"

Alex laughed. "I have to admit, I really do not want to go through the portal again. The prospect terrifies me. But I will do it for Shirl or Candy."

"Frankly, I would rather have you stay here. You said you were starting to get headaches, back on Ginkgo Terra. After the pounding your poor head took yesterday, I think it prudent it is not exposed to the Gingko Terra atmosphere. Originally Shirl was going to be the first one to come over. Darden and I will get her through the portal." Alex was relieved with Tarsea's answer.

"I can meet with her family while you get her. They will probably want to know a little about Shirl before they meet her. Do they live here in the Aster Province? Can she stay here in Tolfer's old room for a little while when she first comes over?"

"I know Mom and Dad would not want Shirl to be anywhere but here when she first arrives," Tarsea replied. "I have no idea where her family lives. Darden was doing this all on his own. I am not even sure he would have mentioned any of this to us. Thank the Supreme Being that you were caught in the stream of the portal."

Alex was once again thankful that things had occurred as they did. Although, she had wished the assassination attempt had not happened. She could not regret for one minute, giving up the life she had in the other world. Her life was here, with her soul mate.

She started to drift back to sleep when Darden's voice came across the warrior channel.

"I do not know how, but Shirl came through the portal. There was an alarm that a gateway was opened and something came through. Two guards were dispatched and found her unconscious. She is being detained at The Palace. I saw them carrying her in a couple of minutes ago."

Tarsea tightened his hold on her. "We will save her, Alex, I promise. Nothing is going to happen to your best friend!"

Alex looked at her soul mate. Dread crept through her body. She would do whatever it took to save her friend.

The End

Enjoy the first chapter of
'The Crystal Telepath'
Book Two of the Worlds Apart Series

Chapter 1

~

Sedona, Arizona

She exited the car, so weak she could barely close the door. The remnants of the second migraine this week had left her feeling lethargic. Shirl Tomlinson knew she had to power through, regardless of how dreadful she was feeling. Her best friend, Alexandra Mann, had been missing for almost a week. As she walked to the front of the Sedona Police Department headquarters, she was oblivious to the beauty of the surrounding area. Several people exiting the building made way for Shirl as she entered. She barely noticed their presence or the way the men perused her body. She was too sick to care.

For a relatively small town, the place was extremely busy. Barely able to stand, she staggered toward the front desk. She had to dodge a number of officers; otherwise, she would have ended up flat on her face on the marble floor. The man who stood behind the counter saw her distress and made his way around the restricted area to aid her. The artificial light was so bright, she had to squint her eyes as she watched him approach.

"Miss Tomlinson, are you all right?" the concerned officer asked. Shirl wished she could remember the young officer's name. He was wearing a name badge, but her vision was blurry and she could not make out the letters. She just wanted to crawl into the corner and fall into a deep, painless sleep.

"I am recovering from a migraine and I am not feeling quite right," she said. One severe headache after another had tapped her strength. She did not know how much more she was going to be able to take. Having only minimal health insurance coverage, her options were limited in her quest to find what was wrong with her. Every doctor she saw scratched their heads, baffled by the escalation at the severity and frequency of the headaches she had been suffering the past two years.

"I'll get Commander Lewis. He will give you an update on our efforts to find your friend." The officer took a couple of steps and then asked over his shoulder, "Can I get you any water?"

Shirl shook her head. She had taken medication before she left the hotel room. Everyone in the Sedona Police Department knew her by now. She arrived on Monday, as soon as she was able to drive. Alex had been missing since last Friday. For three full days, the police station had been her home away from home.

She sat on the bench, clasping the crystals that hung around her neck. As each day ended with no sign of Alex, Shirl got more frantic, fearing she would never see her friend again. What would she do without Alex in her life? They had grown up together in a Phoenix orphanage. Whenever anything went wrong, she always ran to Alex for help. Although Alex was two years younger, Alex was always the responsible one.

Commander Lewis appeared and sat next to Shirl. He was a good looking man, probably in his late thirties. The man was also tall. Generally she had to look up at him when they talked, she liked that. For some odd reason, she did not trust men she had to look down upon. She knew that was stupid, but that was how she felt.

Lewis was the second highest ranking police officer in the department, under the chief of police. Shirl could see from the expression on his face, he did not have good news to share. At least they hadn't found a body. The last two nights Shirl had woken in a cold sweat, dreaming she'd been taken to the morgue to identify Alex's corpse.

"I don't know what to tell you, Miss Tomlinson. There have been no sightings of your friend. We know she checked into her hotel Friday afternoon and was not seen again. Her car was found in a parking lot near Boynton Canyon. We believe she went hiking, but there are no signs of foul play. We have had men up and down that canyon looking for Alexandra. There was a part of the trail that looked like someone was dragged for ten feet or so, but there is no evidence she fell. Why don't you head home? I'll call you if we discover anything."

Shirl felt tears falling down her cheeks and reached into her purse for a tissue. "I can't leave here without Alex or knowing what happened to her." People did not just disappear off the face of the Earth. Sedona seemed an unlikely place for human trafficking. A new age cult, perhaps, but Alex wasn't the type.

"Can I at least take you to dinner? You look terrible." Shirl had to smile at Commander Lewis's comment. Men usually fawned over her. It was nice to have a man be honest with her about her appearance. He was a no nonsense guy, saying what was on his mind.

She didn't feel threatened by him. Commander Lewis was the type of man to drag his wife along, eliminating any type of impropriety. It would be nice to get her mind off Alex, even for one meal. "That would be nice. I can't remember the last time I ate." She had a couple of power bars in her car, but hadn't been able to stomach the idea of eating them.

"Why don't I pick you up tonight in your hotel lobby after I get off, around seven." The seasoned police officer knew this meet-up location would be non-threatening compared to meeting her at her hotel room. "My wife Carol will meet us at the restaurant." Yup, she called that one right!

"I guess at this point, I should at least ask your first name," Shirl said. "It would be weird calling your wife Carol while calling you Commander Lewis."

"Frank, my first name is Frank."

Commander Lewis patted her hand and returned to work. She watched as he crossed into the restricted area behind the front desk. A large clock displayed three o'clock. She had four hours to kill before he would pick her up. There was no sense staying on the hard bench. She could get an update at dinner tonight. Besides, they had her cell phone number if they found Alex in the meantime.

Shirl walked to her car and sat behind the wheel for a while, not sure where she wanted to go. The medication had kicked in and she felt a little better.

She started toward Boynton Canyon. Shirl rarely went hiking with Alex. She didn't like the dust that covered her on the few occasions she went. Alex didn't make a big deal out of having to go alone.

Generally their friend Candy was along and she would hike with Alex. Candy had grown up in the orphanage with them. It was hard not calling her to join Shirl in Sedona while she waited for news of Alex. Candy was a high school coach and her team had just returned from a tournament. She hadn't even told

Candy that Alex was missing. Shirl didn't want to worry her friend in case Alex reappeared. That possibility continued to slip away.

When she arrived, the parking lot was relatively empty. Alex's disappearance had been all over the local newspapers. People were shying away from this particular trail, afraid a wild animal had attacked her friend. There was no evidence to support the claim, but that did not stop the rumor mill from spreading that story.

Boynton Canyon was beautiful with its deep red rocks. Shirl had always been fascinated by this place. It was one of the four vortexes Sedona was famous for. The energy emitted by the vortexes always renewed her.

These sites were believed to be multiple dimensional pathways emitting spiraling spiritual energy. Shirl soaked up any article on the subject as well as anything dealing with mystical powers.

One of the few items she had from her birth mother was an amethyst crystal that started her fascination with crystals and healing stones. She wore four to five crystals a day, depending on her mood. Her mother's amethyst was the only crystal she wore constantly. It seemed to balance her in some odd way. Shirl felt less alone, like having family close by. She knew it was stupid, but maybe one day it would lead her to some discovery of who she was meant to be.

Curiosity about the section of the trail with the drag mark Commander Lewis mentioned got the better of Shirl. Grabbing a power bar, she started toward the trailhead. She'd walk the path Alex had taken when she disappeared. If she got too dusty, she'd take a shower before Frank picked her up for dinner.

She walked slowly, conserving what strength she had. Between nibbling on the nutrition bar, the medication, and the vortex's energy, she felt vitality coursing through her body. As she walked the trail, she held onto her crystals, trying to channel Alex. She was not expecting anything to happen, then her mother's amethyst started to glow.

Shirl held the crystal in front of her and stared at it in wonder. As much as she knew about crystals, she had never read anything about them glowing. She felt a slight pull and stopped.

The air ahead shimmered and she felt the continued emission of energy. Slowly, she approached the anomaly. She could see the trail on the other side of the air displacement.

Shirl looked down and noticed the dirt and foliage along the path looked as if something had been dragged along it. It ended right in front of what she could only think was an event horizon. Alex must have been pulled through the point of no return. The gravitational pull would have been so great, Alex would not have been able to escape from it.

Taking a deep breath, Shirl walked into the unknown.

⌒○

Inside a black void, she felt as if falling. Twisting and turning, she had no control. Deafening, high-pitched sound pierced her ears. Her crystal glowed brighter.

Terror taking hold, she attempted to grab her crystal necklace. After her second attempt at regaining use of her flailing arms, she secured the amethyst in her hand.

Just short of all-out panic, she started to think about home. It worked for Dorothy in Oz, allowing her and Toto to return to Kansas.

She crashed against the ground, out of the portal's grasp. Shirl slowly climbed to her feet and realized she was no longer in Sedona. It must have been a portal to another dimension. That could be the only explanation why she was no longer on the trail surrounded by red rocks and dirt.

She stood on a mountain path, overlooking a city built of pale stone. The community was abloom with purple flowering trees and plants. The violet sky must be a result of the colored pollen emitted.

Shirl was surprised her mind was reacting rationally, although she was still a little dazed. Her normal reaction would have been to panic. Instead, she took in her surroundings and making scientific assumptions. She could not remember the last time she had thought so clearly. There was no pain or pressure impacting her brain.

Alexandra was somewhere in this city, she was certain of it. Shirl was not sure how she was going to find her or what type of people she would encounter. But she had to start looking.

She started down the mountain pass, paying close attention to her steps. The trail was steeper than the one in Boynton Canyon. Her sandals were comfortable, but not equipped to traverse the rocky path. She was also a little wobbly from the rough ride within the portal and had eaten no food to speak of for days.

Sweat trickled down her neck. She brushed at the liquid and her hand came back covered in blood. Shirl felt the same trickle on the other side of her neck. She was bleeding from both ears.

Another step. Bright red streamed from her nose. Her shirt collar was soaked with blood. A strong wave of nausea washed over her. She grabbed a tree branch along the trail.

Leaning on the tree did not abate the nausea. She fell to her knees and retched along the side of the trail. With little food and nothing to drink, it was closer to dry heaves.

Voices and footsteps were coming closer. Eyes popping open, she glanced through a red haze. Not only was she bleeding from her ears and nose, blood vessels must have broken in her eyes.

Shirl could hear the two men address her, but could not comprehend what they said. Her ears were buzzing and she could barely concentrate through the nausea that still overwhelmed her. One of the men knelt next to her as she felt herself fall into unconsciousness.

About the Author

When Evelyn Lederman retired from her career as an insurance executive, she cheerfully anticipated the freedom to finally spend as much time reading as she'd always wanted. The twist in her story came when as-yet unwritten characters started cropping up in her thoughts, asking her to tell their stories. Now, she spends her days in Florida on the beach...with her laptop.

The Chameleon Soul Mate is the first book in her paranormal romance series, Worlds Apart.

Contact me at evelynlauthor@gmail.com, her website: evelynlederman. com, or Facebook at Evelyn Lederman, Author. Make sure to like my Amazon Author page. You can sign-up for my newsletter through my web-site. Saw hi to me on Twitter and Goodreads, as well.